What's the matter, girl?

For Joan with
best wishes

Elizabeth
Bergmann

What'

the matter, girl?

Elizabeth Brochmann

HARPER & ROW, PUBLISHERS

NEW YORK

Cambridge
Hagerstown
Philadelphia
San Francisco

1817

London
Mexico City
Sao Paulo
Sydney

What's the Matter, Girl?

Copyright © 1980 by Elizabeth Brochmann

All rights reserved. No part of this book may be used or reproduced in
any manner whatsoever without written permission except in the case of
brief quotations embodied in critical articles and reviews. Printed in the
United States of America. For information address Harper & Row,
Publishers, Inc., 10 East 53rd Street, New York, N.Y. 10022. Published
simultaneously in Canada by Fitzhenry & Whiteside Limited, Toronto.

Library of Congress Cataloging in Publication Data
Brochmann, Elizabeth.
    What's the matter, girl?

    SUMMARY: Thirteen-year-old Anna contends with
members of her unusual family as she awaits the
return of her uncle from years away at the war.
    [1. Emotional problems—Fiction. 2. World War,
1939–1945—Fiction] I. Title.
PZ7.B78085Wh   [Fic]   79–2022
ISBN 0-06-020677-2
ISBN 0-06-020678-0 lib. bdg.

FIRST EDITION

For my dad, Jack Luckhurst
(1910–1970)

Many have helped me with my writing—none more than my editor, Elaine Edelman. I wish to thank her, my husband, Hal, and our children: Kari, Mike, Craig; and my good friends: Jutta, Meg, Margaret, Alan, Anne, Charlotte, Pegs, Eugene, Button, Roger, Susan, Charles, Sally, and Sandra. Also I am indebted to fellow writers of the North Shore Writer's Club: Beth, John, Bill, and Suzanne especially. My thanks to the Canadian writers who have generously supported me: George Ryga, Lionel Kearns, and Jack Hodgins. To all these good friends and to the good people of the Canada Council, I wish to say 'thank you' in this, my first book.

Homecoming Minus 7

"What's the matter, girl? Anna! You going to sit on those porch steps till the world ends?" Gran scolds from the kitchen doorway, wiping her hands on her blue apron. Bird tiny, swift moving, sharp spoken, she's always wearing blue, sky-blue and navy-blue. Gramps says her hair is salt-and-pepper; I say it's granite. Gramps calls her his Jaybird; I call her "Yes-Gran, No-Gran, Whatever-you-say-Gran."

But I am going to sit here the whole day—a whole week if I want to. Maybe. Why doesn't the Jaybird leave me alone? Why does she have to catch me like this with my head between my knees, rocking, rocking, Uncle Arion's name . . . Arion Arion Arion . . . echoing in my head? I stop and stare at the top of my bobby socks.

"Answer me, girl!"

Sometimes I think it's surprising we all love her. Her

and her sharp bird's tongue. I lift up just a little, enough to see my feet in saddle shoes.

"Wastin' time! Sit up! You're rocking like a child!"

"Yes, Gran." I unroll.

"Leave her, hey Maw," calls Gramps from his giant chair in the lightest corner of the dark kitchen. "No harm in just sitting on the porch, is there?" She *hrrumps*, and he pats her blue-flowered rump as she swoops on past into the pantry. Gramps knows I'm waiting; I've been waiting over four years now—not on this very porch— but I've been waiting one, two, three, four years, waiting for my uncle Arion to come back. Gramps leans back and turns his huge silvery lion's head to stare out the wavery glass of the kitchen window, through the plum trees, over the field to my mom and dad's house, and straight on through the mountains that rim our valley, beyond our island and over the ocean, maybe all the way to Germany where he was born. His thinning mane floats, hair and beard—and, oh, how I do love him, my gramps.

Gran chirps bird whistles as if she's done nothing wrong in bothering me. I frown at her back, silent of course—she turns on me, and I'm forced to smile. Sullen, I squeeze our dog Boy sitting here beside me. He whines. If Gran is angry or hurt, I don't care. I don't want to think about or feel for anybody but me.

I can see scraps of blue sky through the shingles that never leak. Gramps won't ever paint this lean-to, I guess, just leave the gray weathered wood tacked onto the flaking white-painted house—"A *shanty*," Gran snaps, "just like a shanty in a shanty-town." But I like it, it's comfortable. The steps are silver, and slivery, so I sit

carefully. And Boy squats beside me, and we sun ourselves in the blue-white morning sun exactly as Uncle
Arion and I sunned ourselves in afternoons four and a
half years ago.

And me whispering my secrets into his ear . . .

"There's a wasps' nest in the hayloft, did you know
that? Did you know the skunk cabbages are out in the
marsh, Uncle Arion? Yesterday did you see the skywrit-
ing over town?"

Gran comes back outside, her apron like a pouch.
"Here, you're doing nothing, play with these. That's
what I did when I was a girl." She empties some of her
stunted yellow potatoes from her apron into my lap. I'm
too old for this! She steps back inside and behind the
door, and takes the toothpicks and colored buttons out
of the sewing drawer of the big pine cabinet that Gramps
built. "Here's some legs and eyes."

I'm much too old for this! "Thank you, Gran." I
frown.

My sixteen year old Aunt Gemma, Gran's pet, comes
up from the cellar with a bucket of spuds and pipes up,
"Look at that! Look at that rude girl! Doesn't she have
a home of her own to go to?" She melts into the gloom
with Gran.

Who does she think she is! She's not so pretty—
skinny-legs-Gemma with her silly painted toes—not
as pretty as her twin, Aunt Ginny. She knows I have a
home—but I've as much right to be here as she does, and
I'm staying!

Boy whimpers, paws at me, trying to get me to
smile and pat him. I just pat him. He's a beauty and   <u>3</u>

useful too, a good bird dog. Gramps says he's the color of prairie wheat in a good year, the wheat he used to grow in pre-Dust Bowl days. Gemma says, "That dog is drab old khaki color." But she lies. Boy's coat is the color of Uncle Arion's hair. Uncle Arion, Cousin Alice, and Boy are the only blondes in the family now that Gramps is gray.

My hair is brown, shot with red 'cause Dad's red-headed, a red-headed high rigger. It's my only vanity, my hair; I'm too plain not to be humble. Dad hates to see me looking in a mirror; he likes his women humble and shy.

I choose the handsomest potato for a body, two long thin ones for legs.

Gramps starts snoring in his giant chair; his size twelve feet in gray work socks are propped on the footstool. ("No point in having a foot unless you have a whole foot," Gramps always says.) One thumb is hooked in his suspenders that hike his old wool fisherman's pants up over his paunch. How can he sleep so much? He is marking time too, just like me.

Two smaller thin potatoes do for the arms. One, unfortunately, is misshapen, but it's the only one thin enough. I stick the wide end of the toothpick into the body and the pointed end into the legs and then do the same with the arms.

The sun shines fat. Gramps' black Manx cat comes out on the stoop and swipes at its fur with a prickly tongue. Boy gives it a friendly sniff, it hisses and arches; Boy's hackles rise but he backs off. A violent-blue Stellar's jay in the plum tree rat-a-tat-tats its machine-gun attack. I give that bird and the cat too a dirty look.

I need a special potato for the head. And what will I use for hair? Marsh comes around the peony bush, "Hey Sis, why the fierce frown?"

"Oh, 'lo Marsh."

"Come gaffing?" My big brother doffs his battered hunting cap, flips his hair back, and slaps the cap back on. He's only a year and a half older—he's fifteen—but he looks out for me. He has black hair like Mom's. "What are you making, Sis?"

"Uncle Arion."

"Want to use my hunting knife?"

There's a fresh cut on his hand, still reddish among the shiny white scars that he gets while skinning the muskrats and mink from off his trapline. The halfmoon scar on the side of his face that he got jumping off Blindman's Bluff shines and will never fade.

"Thanks." The knife's a good idea. I can drill eyes, cut a mouth, maybe. I fix Arion's head to his body; it twists sideways a bit and looks a little odd.

"Why not come gaffing with me?"

"I don't feel like it."

"Oh, okay."

Arion looks like he's standing at attention like a soldier. I pull out one leg and set it back so he's standing at ease.

"Know what you can use for hair, Sis?"

"No, what?"

"Boy's fur."

Boy wags his tail. We look at him and laugh. "That's a good idea, Marsh." And we pet him.

Marsh lifts off his cap, sits down, and hangs it on his

knee and runs a hand through his own black hair. "You okay?" Marsh frowns at me.

"Sure. I guess."

He looks down his long legs at the cut in his rubber boots. "Don't start in worrying, eh Sis."

It's not like him to show he cares, and I don't know what to answer.

Boy runs around him, bouncing, anxious to be off on the glassy river, gaffing the silvery-blue salmon spotted red and white with rot. Boy loves dragging them out of the shallows into the tall rushes and saw grass or up into the bush by himself. There he can hide and eat until he's bloated. We're always having to scold him, for the dead fish are supposed to be fertilizer for Mom's garden. When we used to ask him, Arion never would come with us, because of the stink.

"You stay, Boy, and keep Sis company," Marsh says gruffly.

But I know he'd like Boy to keep him company. He strides off, and I see for the first time how he's built like Uncle Arion. But Marsh has black hair and straightforward eyes, and Uncle Arion's eyes under his sun-yellow hair are changeable.

Boy whines beside me, then collapses and drools in the heat, panting and swatting his tail so that the dust rises in tiny clouds from between the unpainted floorboards. I give him a squeeze. I'm glad Marsh let him stay!

It was Arion who rescued Boy from the pound for us seven years ago.

I sit up, stretch my legs straight, and splay them

open, my arms out too; my hands dangle limp from my wrists; I exhale all my wind. I do that on hot, close days, and today is a real sticky one. Mount Arrow's snowcap has melted this year. Our valley, lidded with a tin sky, is hot and sticky as a soft-boiled egg.

My brother waves from across the browning field, behind him the river shimmers, beyond that, mirages quaver on the mud flats. Boy sees him and whimpers to be off, but I hold him down by his collar and wave to Marsh to show that I'm definitely not coming. I feel like sending Boy after him, but Marsh might think I'm ungrateful and I couldn't hurt my brother.

As for the rest of them, I don't care what the family says. I'm staying! I'll sit right here from breakfast till supper every day till Uncle Arion finally comes home to Canada from wherever he is now. Nobody's going to talk me out of it, even though it's more than a year since I had a letter. It's where we used to sit, Uncle Arion and I, the sun shining through his fuzzy hair in a halo—yellow hair frizzed up no matter how much he greased it down.

It's going to be great when he gets back—the way it always was.

I can see him back then, lying there in the short grass that he and Gramps have just scythed, flat on his back under the biggest greengage plum tree, his knees drawn up and one foot propped; lying there dreaming on the clouds. But that was over four years ago when I was only nine. He was eighteen. A long time ago. Before he went off to Hitler's war.

I lay my potato figure on its back. It will be my gift

to Arion, this potato man. When he comes back from wherever he is—but I don't ask where he is.

He got up then, and came and sat with me on the porch step. "Hi, how's my nine-year-old, nine-hundred-pound ugly duck?" Uncle Arion tweaked my braid.

I didn't like him calling me that.

"How's my fairy princess?"

Oh, but I loved that!

"Want a ride?"

"Yes, yes, Uncle Arion!" He clasped his fingers together, making me a stirrup. I heaved myself onto his back and off we went, pounding down the path, hoofing over the grass under the apple trees, confetti petals falling, galloping, galloping, oh, it was fun, it was fun, it was such fun. My braids flapping, we headed straight for the fence . . . "Oh oh oh" I could feel the boniness of his shoulders . . . and veered off, my braids snapping, heading east then to the blossoming cherry trees and down the aisles of gooseberry and currant bushes—then suddenly west again and I waved to a friend coming out of the reserve down River Road—east again, down river toward the canal and the docks . . . his hair a golden cloud under my chin—his body warm under me. Then it was south to the river and—oooh—sharply back north, a braid slapping my face . . . oh what fun . . . toward the field with the farms beyond that lay this side of Beaver Road. He pumped his elbows, and his shoulder blades cut into my chest. I lifted my head and my hair loosened, falling like a veil over my eyes; I threw back my head laughing; my eyes lifted to the mountains, up up past the logging slashings that marred our hills, up up to the steeple of Mount Arrow's peak. My Arion, my uncle Arion! We leaned over and he snatched me a bouquet of parsley. My legs slipped and I felt his ribs before I righted myself.

Then we went thundering on, my steed Arion and I the rider, up the path to Gran and Gramps' toy house painted white, trimmed red—and on past Gran carrying in vegetables for spring-garden soup; "You're driving that child hysterical, son," and I went shrieking by.

Gramps' two cows, one brown, the other white, in the back field looked up stupidly still chewing their cuds, as with a shrill whinny, Arion charged. Buttercup flew off kicking herself in the udder, which hung like full pink fingers. Daisy stopped chewing, blinked.

I laughed and laughed. "Let me stroke her, Arion. Come, Buttercup, poor girl." She was bawling, but more from insult than injury. She headed for her stall in the milking shed by the barn.

Arion swore, "Shit and goddamn," and dumped me in the tall grass, and waved me invisible with his long bony fingers. Only my feelings were hurt. "Dad'll have my skin . . . I forgot to milk her . . . he'll have kittens— a whole damn litter and my hide too, if he sees that bloated bag." And his lips grew thinner and bluer, and his nose grew sharper as it always did when he was scared.

"It's still quite early," I said to make him feel better. "It's not even lunchtime yet. And you're not afraid of Gramps, are you? Gran will stick up for you." Gran always spoiled him, giving him more than his share of sugar and sweets. But he headed for the barn, swearing.

Two barn kittens were playing in the shadows of the slat door; they skittered off when he stomped past, letting the shed door slap shut behind him. A whiff of cow dung hit me, and I breathed out sharply. I heard the cow peeing. I peeked through a crack in the door; her tail was arched up at the root and her pee was spraying, fanning out of the trough onto the manured floorboards, making them wet and slippery. I backed off and stroked a mother barn cat as she came up. Arion was holding his nose. I heard him give a swat, heard Buttercup moo and the milk pail clatter as she kicked it. "Dumb damn cow!" I heard a thud and her grunt. Poor Buttercup.

Out in the field Daisy chewed her cud contentedly. Her bag was not so swollen because she was slowly drying up. Arion was leery of her, for she stepped on him whenever she could, then shifted all her weight onto that foot. He would curse then and push; she would blink and chew, three legs at rest.

I heard more barn kittens playing above in the loft and I climbed up to look for them. They were tumbling around Gramps' giant bear trap, stored in a dark corner. "A lethal weapon," Gramps called it. "Could take a man's leg right off," he'd say to me, smiling strangely. "Stay away from it, Pet."

I heard the mother barn cats mewing below me, begging Arion as milk clamored in the bottom of the pail, then hissed softly as it filled. I hoped Arion was not in too foul a mood to squirt milk into their open mouths. I didn't always understand his moods.

10

I was staring at the trap when Arion called out. I liked looking at Gramps' bear trap and imagining blood and gore and a raging bear—and me, safe of course, just out of reach of its jaws. Arion clapped his hands, "Anna! Looking at the trap, Anna?" I could tell from the sound of his voice that he was grinning, knew he guessed my private gory thoughts. I realized I'd been smiling strangely.

I hollered back, "No, I'm not!" Why does he tease me? Why does he change from gentle to teasing-mean, guessing at my forbidden excitement, my secrets? Gramps wouldn't like the violent trap pictures in his gentle granddaughter's mind.

I don't like them either.

Arion came to the bottom of the ladder, "Hey kid, sorry I dumped you. You okay?"

"Yes, I'm fine"—now. He's back to being himself.

"Good. You can have the froth off the milk when I'm finished."

I loved the froth. From the loft window I watched Arion go out in the field calling, "Moo Coo, Moo Coo." Daisy looked up and plopped a pie.

One of the mother cats, the one Arion favored a little, climbed up the ladder crooning to her kittens. Untangling themselves from the straw and each other, running, falling over themselves, the kittens came to suckle.

There were two litters at one time. That meant too many cats. I looked away, and I knew Arion was cussing softly. The other cat's newborn litter moved blindly in the nest, mewing shrilly. They didn't know that Gramps would make Arion drown them with a stone and a sack in our river.

One evening Arion and I swam alone together in the smooth green Kitsucksis River. . . .

"Stop that or else!" I cried.

"Or else what, you little mud puppy. This is the shark you're wrassling with."

"Get off me!" The green water swallowed me, and I swallowed the green water before I surfaced.

"Hey, aren't you ever going to get too old for braids?" He gave a yank.

"Let me go." He'd pinned my arms behind my back and drawn my head up by my hair. I waited . . . my head craned down river; the river flowed into the salty canal . . . I waited . . . the river flowed on out to the blue-black ocean.

Then I squirmed and flailed about in the water and weeds. He grinned and forced my face down till I felt I'd drown. I gave up, then floated very still and tried to hold my breath.

"Or else what, my ugly duckling?" And he laughed. "Still waters run . . . run . . ." He tugged on my braid and waited for me to answer his old quip—"Still waters run???"

"Stupid." I winced.

He grinned. But he didn't let me up, not until he felt like it. "Cry uncle."

But now I see it as kind of funny. I guess.

"What are you laughing at, Anna!" It's my other

twin aunt, my favorite, Aunt Ginny. She's pretty, except that she has Gramps' big nose. Ginny and Gemma are sweet sixteen, lucky stiffs. She balances on one long leg like a flamingo. She's dressed in pink. She runs a hand through her hair that's brushed till it shines—but it's only brown.

"Oh, nothing."

"What's the matter, Pet?"

"Nothing really, Ginny, I . . ."

Ginny, rubbing the side of her nose, her bad habit, dances on past me into the kitchen where Gran stands working . . . before I can catch my breath and say more. "What's bothering Anna? She's not herself? . . . I had such a lovely time. . . ."

Regularly I used to ask, "When's Arion coming home?" until Ginny told me to drop it. I didn't ask her why. . . .

One week to the homecoming. I don't know where he's coming from, but he'll land in Vancouver, then he'll take the ferry to our island. And then it will be the train home here to Port Salish. I want Uncle Arion to find me right where he left me, on the stoop with Boy. I'm going to stay here no matter what anybody says. No one—not ugly Gemma, not Uncle Barnard, or Aunt Cessy, or Aunt Lud, or Cousin Alice, not even my own dear Ginny or brother Marsh—can talk me out of it. I won't care where he's been or why he's forgotten me—just so long as he comes home.

I'd sleep here in my old khaki army bag that's stained orange and I'd wish on the North Star, if they'd let me. There are always things I can't do and things people won't tell me. "Why is that bag stained orange, Dad?" I asked once. "What, Anna? Oh that. Well I guess it's . . . uh . . . medicine." "Medicine, Dad?" "Iodine maybe. Now run along and play, honey." "You mean a wounded soldier slept in this bag?" Dad didn't answer me; there are things people just won't tell a "little girl"!

"Anna, stop lazing on that stoop and come in here and peel the carrots!" Gemma yells.

I don't budge.

"Leave her be," says Gramps. "She's a good girl."

"Humph!"

"Hey Maw, what time is it?" Gramps calls from his chair.

"Near noon," Gran calls back.

"Grumph. Exactly what time!" Gramps grumphs and then mumbles. "Hasn't a man the right to the exact time!" Gramps' eyesight is failing so he can't read his pocket watch; he stretches it out at arm's length toward the light from the window, and he squints. "Getting old, arms are shrinking." He's always calling out for the time these days, in his own language, *Was ist die Uhr?*

I'm waiting too as I stare out over the flat summer river and the mud flats to the wall of mountains. Marsh, Arion, and I used to sit here, talking, dreaming together.

"What's eating Anna?"

I hear them discussing me . . . and I don't like it. People better mind their own business or else.

"What you making, Anna?" Gemma hollers from the kitchen.

"Potatoes."

Homecoming Minus 6

Gemma talks loudly in the kitchen—she wants me to overhear her. "If you ask me she's behaving like a spoiled brat, sitting there, pouting on those steps like there's some magic in sitting where she used to sit with her favorite uncle." Gemma wrinkles her nose and raises her voice and wiggles her butt. "Like it'll bring Arion back whole and safe. She's like a little kid who's lost her sucker! Somebody ought to tell her what's going on."

Nobody asked you, Gemma. I should tell her that. I should shout at her that I don't care that he's forgotten me, just so long as he comes home. But I just glare through the doorway. Why has he forgotten me? What does she mean "whole"? Why isn't he home? It's over a year since the war ended. I won't ask.

"I still say somebody ought to tell her. Even her 15

mom and dad say she should think more about the real
world."

"Now, Gemma." Gramps wags a finger. "Anna is a
good girl. You leave her be. . . . Sometimes it feels good
to be a child again. You can ask me; I know." Gramps
heaves a big sigh.

Poor Gramps. Good old Gramps. "She's still
young," he says, like it's a fine thing to be young. He
nods asleep. But I'm not so young; I'll be a junior at
Salish High this year. I was only nine and a half when
Arion left.

Three potato figures of Arion lean against the post.
And I'm working on one of me, riding on his back, my
face lost in a cloud of Boy's borrowed hair.

Arion is my favorite person in the whole world.
When I was feeling low, he'd say, "Come, princess,
you're in a glass coffin. I'll awake you with a kiss." And
he'd kiss the end of my nose or kiss the tip of my braid
and flip it over my shoulder. We would laugh. And then
he'd listen. I even told him how I feared the coming of
the "curse," and he said, "Why then, princess, you'll be
a queen." But he blushed. We were chums. And he con-
fessed to me, "Some girls scare me, Anna, scare me
shitless." I shivered.

"Isn't she a little old for playing with those potatoes?" Gemma says loudly, so I'll be sure to hear her.

Sometimes I hate my whole family . . . well everybody but Arion and Gramps . . . and Marsh . . . and maybe
a few others. I love Mom and Dad of course, but they're
not as important to me, somehow, not like they were
when I was little.

Pretty soon everybody's going to start arriving for the celebration of Uncle Arion's homecoming; all Gran and Gramps' children and their mates: crabby Uncle Barnard; Aunt Ludmilla and Uncle Hudson, whom everyone calls Lud and Hud; Aunt Cessy, who's married to my quiet uncle Jerry and who'll be dressed like a carnival for the glory of Uncle Arion's homecoming. Gramps will be playing his jokes again. When everybody's assembled in the front parlor and there's a little pause, Gramps will start clearing his throat and fumbling in his pockets. "Hey Maw, you gotch the family denchures?" He always does that on formal occasions.

I hope it's glorious.

I won't help with the preparations. If anyone asks me, I'll say I'm busy. No, I'll say no. I look at my hands prattling on my knees like they don't belong to me. That used to be Arion's habit, prattling fingers on his knees . . . I try to pretend they are his fingers on my knees.

It's over a year since I got a letter and I've written him faithfully and that's not fair. Now they say he's coming home, but still he hasn't written me.

Rrrrrruff. Boy squirms at my feet and growls.

"Isn't that right, Boy? Not fair?"

Boy, Marsh, Arion, and I, we used to canoe together on our river. But once Arion and I went out alone in the late evening when the blue-black sky had turned the color of the blue-black river. He touched my hand on my knee. "You're a pretty girl."

I watch those hands of mine on my knees drift away from me; then I call them back. They are not pretty hands, these strong fingers and square nails, so like Dad's; a man's hands.

I was ugly when Uncle Arion left me. But I'm a little better now. I'm never pretty; I've flat feet and freckles and a double-jointed thumb. When I was nine, I called myself the Chameleon Kid, because my eyes wander, any direction, one at a time. My feet turn in a bit too. All that was fun when I was not yet ten, but now that I'm nearly fourteen I know it's ugly. I guess I'm not truly ugly—just especially ordinary. I don't like my eyes, my feet, my nose, my freckles; my shoulders are broad and my hips too wide. I only hope someday a man will find me extraordinarily lovely, and then we'll be in love. For now I'm just me with one uncle who tells pretty lies. And another uncle who doesn't . . . Uncle Barnard, firstborn of Gran's brood, big boss, says I'm a homely muffin! Gramps says I'm an ordinary girl with the heart and soul of a poet . . . like any ordinary girl. It's all nonsense.

I wore braids then, when Arion left, and I sat a lot even then, and grew plumper. I'm thinner now and wear my hair hanging loose. Even so, I take after the square side of Mom's family. It was always Arion running easily and me hobbling along at his heel. Me, a lump, with a foot turned in and an eye turned out. I'm a little prettier now, but still I'm not Gladys! Oh she wasn't all that pretty—but Arion wasn't really asking me, or any of us then, how we felt about Gladys.

I couldn't have told him.

Him with his blonde hair, blue eyes, and wild ways—a rainbow after the rain. Arion the Prince—and at the same time just flesh and blood like any of us unkissed frogs.

Sometimes I think he'd rather play with little girls, little girls like me. Except for Gladys. He met her just before he left for boot camp. All dressed up in his khaki uniform with brass buttons and puttees and his sunshine hair hidden under his cap and his eyes as blue as Oyster Shell Bay on a brilliant day, he marched left right, left right, right out of my life and off to war. And no one's telling where he is now.

All I know is that I wait for letters that never arrive anymore and he is so far away. And who knows where he is now. No, I don't really ask.

It seems so long ago.

The trees, brush, and fields were pure black. We paddled the canoe out to mid-river and floated, suspended. Arion and I, caught in mid-flight. I turned myself upside down in my mind. It was easy to do, because the land was mirrored in the water and so were the stars.

Arion leaned forward, patted my knee. "You're pretty, Anna, a pretty girl."

It was a lie.

He leaned back. "Want to go roller skating tomorrow?"

Oh yes! "Yes, thank you."

And next day we went.

I was struggling to keep my balance in the current of skaters when he came up behind me. "Hey Anna, want a ride?"

The floor was green as the river, slippery as the mossy rock bed. The lights were the too-bright brightness of the hottest day reflecting off the water and burning your eyes. The ceiling was high, high up like the sky, the rafters rang with shouting, and my head ached.

He hoisted me up on his shoulders, my wheels spinning, and we skimmed across the roller rink, swooping in circles, the board walls blurring. My favorite uncle, my favorite horse, my unicorn!

"Young man," the speaker blared, "you with the girl on your shoulders! That's against the rules."

Arion took his time slowing down, then he bowed. "Yes sir, yes sir." To me he said, "Stupid rule! Who ever heard of a rule says you can't carry your girl on your shoulders!" He winked and sped off, leaving me standing there with everyone whirling around me so fast it was frightening. Joe, my brother's friend, slammed into me, "Sorry sorry! . . . Oh, it's only you."

After a bit I got back into the swim. Up ahead I could see Arion whirling in circles, his arm under a girl who was leaning backward, like movie stars do before they kiss, her hair floating. I hated her so much I could hardly breathe. A little later she rolled my way, leaned over, and whispered to me, "Your uncle Arion is a rare one, a gentleman and an animal."

I glowered, "You leave my uncle alone!" She skated off backward, smirking. I hated him then, right after I had loved him best of all.

He left his partner, still unkissed, and the other girls swirled around him, rolling at breakneck speed, caught <u>20</u> in the current. Their wheels blurred, they whirled and eddied, their voices grew shrill; one girl, hanging on, cracked at the end of the whip and shrieked. Arion slowed, then stopped, leaning against the backboard, beached. The girls swam to him, swarmed around him, fluttering, giggling. When it got too close for comfort, he stretched his arms out and flew off like some tropical fish not found in Kitsucksis River. "Hey, hey, you girls are all too much for me. We got enough pushy women in the family as it is."

He winked and smiled at me as if to say "except for you, Anna." And he skated off from them and their siren songs. I stood and watched. Half the time I couldn't see Arion. Then I saw him.

He rolled straight across the rink against the traffic with a string of girls behind him. Once his sister Gemma had yelled, "Awwh Don Juan, it's all an act with you!" He had turned red but said nothing. He should have socked her right between the eyeballs.

Then that animal-loving starlet bore down on me, "You're sure not good-looking like your uncle, are you!" and before I could answer, hurled on by, sticking her tongue out. A guy waltzed sideways to her, "Hey Gladys!" What an ugly name!

The next day the river flooded. My brother said, "Wow, what a flood! Let's go get Arion, Sis."

"Okay." We reached our skiff, which the river had floated into our yard.

"You pole while I paddle," he said.

"Okay." I gave a push, and we floated toward the flooded hollow.

Mom, her back to us, was wearing hip-waders, gathering up the garbage that floated out of the can. "Hey May, my sensible Mayfly" Dad always calls her.

"Push harder."

I leaned harder on the pole and we skimmed over the fence, enjoying the strangeness of it.

"Harder."

"I can't, it's too deep." I could see the barbed wire wavering beneath us.

We saw Dad walking calmly in gum boots down the submerged River Road, toward City Hall. There he would talk about a dike to the officials and, in case they didn't listen, he'd talk to the newspaper and radio reporters about the politicians' promised dike. What a hullabaloo there would be.

Marsh paddled and I looked for fish swimming over the grass. I didn't see any. I didn't expect to, still I was disappointed. We tied up to a plum tree on the highest ground at Gran and Gramps', stepped out onto the water-covered green grass, grinning, and mounted the porch to go get Arion.

"Dumb cat." Marsh scratched Gramp's Manx cat, but it just sat staring stonily. What was it thinking of, drowned mouse holes? It starchily ignored the scolding jays and chittering songbirds sitting safely in the branches of the plum trees or strung out along the telephone wires. It eyed, instead, the flooding river.

Maybe the earth was like this in prehistoric times, before the Ice Age killed everything dead all at once. Arion once told us that a mastodon was found frozen in a cave near here with a wad of grass in its mouth.

"Let's get Arion."

We opened the door without knocking, because nothing happened at Gran and Gramps' that we weren't allowed to see or would want to miss out on.

Gran snapped. *"Fermez la* door." Close the door. *"Il fait froid."* It's cold outside.

Gramps smiled, *"Willkommen, meine Lieben,"* from his big chair where he was sitting watching the flooded fields. *Welcome my dear grandchildren.* I climbed into the arm of his great chair and started combing his silver hair. Gramps started in spinning his silver tales.

". . . that sea monster took to snarling at me regular. Hid herself every time I chugged into that bay . . ." telling us a fish story we'd heard a thousand times before.

"Where's Arion?" Marsh asked.

"Asleep," Gemma said, "and no wonder. Out carousing all night with that Gladys!"

"Hush, girl!" Gran snapped.

"It's true," Gemma whined.

". . . the shadow of my bow was right over her . . ." Gramps' eyes shone. "She was lying on her back, rolling with the swells, and I'd swear she was smiling like a seal. OUCH. Careful, Anna!"

"Sorry, Gramps, a knot."

"Haven't you combed enough for today, child?"

The Manx cat sat on the other arm of Gramps' giant chair, its back to me. Gramps kept rubbing it behind the ears with his lumpy fingers. A lost soul, that Manx, it just wandered in one day and adopted him and ignored all the rest of us. It sat there looking highly annoyed at the floodwaters. I think it was born annoyed.

I gave Gramps a new style, parting his hair in the

middle and combing it down toward his ears.

"*Mein Gott!* You make me look like Hitler," and he mussed his hair.

"Sorry, Gramps."

"Hope that salt water backing up from the canal won't ruin my flowers," Gran grumbled.

"Arion coming down, do you think?" Marsh asked.

"Act of God." Gramps grinned, cheery once more. ". . . I ever tell you about those whales," he brightened, "escaped from Noah's ark?"

"No Gramps." I liked pulling the comb gently through his thin hair. He never let me comb his beard.

"Well now! You wouldn't want to miss that one."

Arion's bedsprings creaked overhead.

"Disgraceful," Gemma growled, "to come wandering in that time of the morning—"

"Hush!" Gran snapped.

He never did come downstairs that time. Marsh and I knew then that he had outgrown us. It made us feel sad.

That evening Arion brought Gladys home to meet Gran and Gramps. I made sure I was there.

"Just look at her, Anna," my uncle said, showing her off. "Isn't she a beauty?" Gladys stood there tossing her hips and her strawberry-blonde hair. "Isn't she the sun, the moon, and the stars, Anna?"

"What about the planets?" I said grumpily. "Oh, Anna, you're a joker." She caught her sharp nails in my hair. "You funny little thing you." She beat her false lashes and flung out her left arm like it was a lever that set off her tinny peals of laughter.

When she laughed, Uncle Arion just smiled like

she'd said something brilliant, and the other men in the family chuckled like it was some secret joke they all knew. Then Uncle Barnard patted Gladys on the rump, and Arion moved her away from him. She smiled up at Uncle Arion, who was all dressed up in his soldier uniform ready to go off to war, but he didn't see her smile 'cause he was busy giving me a strange little look that said, "Don't be mad, I still love you," or something as stupid. I turned my back. Ginny grinned through it all, but Gemma and my mom and most of the women were watching Gran. Gran was ignoring silly Gladys and staring stonily at the flypaper that hung from the middle of the ceiling, all stuck with the blue-black bodies of summer flies.

Gramps fumbled in his pockets. "Hash anyone gotch the familee denchures?" He grinned at Gran, showing off his gums. "Hey Maw, you gotch the teesh?"

Gladys laughed her alarm-clock laugh.

Even if the whole world forgets, I'll never forgive Gladys for what she did to my Arion.

I make another potato Arion and a potato Gladys with a potato me between them. But then I take us apart because I don't like people to know secret things about me.

Except for Arion. I told him so many secrets!

What if he told her?

I stare out over Gramps' fields and the road. The river, like a looking glass, reflects the birds that dip and skim over its wavering summer skin. Breaths of hot wind ruffle the grassy banks. The grass on the far flats is green: feather clouds, green grass, blue sky, but all of it's a lie because Arion is somewhere far away at war . . . no not at war, the war is over—lost—no, not lost—just lost to me. Why isn't he home with us? The mountains fence us in.

Why isn't it like it used to be?

The mountains are our fence.

It seems like one day he was here and the next day he was gone forever.

Homecoming Minus 5

"How's your potato menagerie?" Gramps calls out from his throne. I lean back in the settling dust, Gran has just swept the porch, and I signal, "Okay, Gramps, okay."

I have three figures of Arion ready for him when he comes marching home. He stands at attention; he stands at ease; he lies on his cot, arms folded like wings.

Bungling Cousin Will comes stumbling up the stairs and gives me a crack on the top of the head with his knuckle. "Won't be long now," he says. I scowl at him. It hurts. "Prince Charming returns," and he winks at me.

Will has no idea of how to dress; today it's green pants, red socks, an old army camouflage shirt, and army boots on his flat feet—and he's feeling sharp! I'd be mad at him for all his silly insinuations if I didn't get the feeling he's more in the dark about Arion than I am.

"Superhuman will soon zoom in for a landing." He grins.

He must be deaf and blind both if he thinks it's going to be like that—even I know better. It's things like that make him still a kid when he's old enough to have gone to war with Arion—if they'd have had him. "Flat feet," they told him. He blushed.

Will walks into the kitchen. "*What* are you wearing?" Gemma laughs.

Poor Will; Gemma's made him blush again.

Will was Arion's sidekick.

One morning years back, I'd snuck up on them. They were hiding under the porch plowing through these old magazines showing sexy girls in slinky black nightgowns and underwear with crazy holes cut out. They were breathing hard. I snuck away, crawling off backward over the cool ground that smelled wet and good.

Another time I remember how they swaggered into the kitchen, doing arm flexes and knee bends, Will copycatting Arion.

"Tish, tish. *Il est un homme musclé!*" Gran shook her head. "A muscleman."

"Want to see a cartwheel, Maw?"

Gramps chuckled, "You want to get so musclebound, son, so every time you take a swig you smash your front teeth in with your beer stein? . . ."

Flex flex, skip skippety skip.

"Why, I remember when I was a young man, like you

and your cousin Will here, and I went to my first *Bier-garten*. My *Mutter* didn't know her son vas . . ."

Arion flashed Gramps a ready grin—"What do you think of this, Maw?"—and he twisted and turned in body-builder poses, Will trying to keep pace.

"My *Mutter*," Gramps raised his voice, "she said to me, 'Helmut, you go to the *Biergarten, ja?*' and—"

"Not bad for a mere mortal, eh, Maw? Watch this."

Gran eyed her sun-god son and clucked like an old hen that had finally laid a double yolker.

"Look at this, Maw. How about our Russian bear dance, Maw!" Will and Uncle Arion crouched and flapped their bent arms, kicked out, flick, flick, a couple of switchblade knives—down through the pantry, right into the middle of the sacred parlor, Will falling behind. They sank then into a dozen slow breathless push-ups. "Ahh haaa ahh haaa . . ."

Everybody's arriving, dressed up fancy for the cele-bration; one at a time they all come by me: an aunt in a cockeyed tam with a feather. "What you doing, Anna?" They're bringing cookies and nuts like it was Christmas of all things; "What you doing, girl?" says a cousin strung in baubles. They're worrying about silly things like the potato salad turning and the entire family dying of ptomaine poisoning. Cousin Alice, a bride-to-be in white lace already, isn't trusted to make potato salad for fear she'll leave the silver spoon in and turn it green. Sometimes I hate my whole family for trying to make everything a joyous celebration. "Up and at 'em, Anna."

"Something wrong with the young one?" asks Aunt Lud, gaunt but ladylike in maroon velvet as she lopes past, smelling of perfumed armpits and cows. I huff behind her back. Her husband, balding and jockey-sized Uncle Hud, is down the road mending his truck with bailing wire.

"Lazy. The young are plain lazy these days," Uncle Barnard, Gran's firstborn, answers her in his tenor voice. He's relaxing on the table bench, eating anything he can grab, like a cream puff that could have been mine. He says, "Hear your aunt call you lazy, Anna?" sneering happily, and I know just squinting his pink-rimmed pig eyes and stroking his chins. Big boss, self-made family general, older by a quarter of a century than my twin aunts.

"What are you scowling at?" asks Cousin Alice, coming past, smiling gently at me, carrying a plate of matrimonial cake. "This is a homecoming. Smile!" She goes inside, her skin is the color of milk. Her eyes and the tiny veins at her temples and on the inside of her upper arms are blue. And on the inside of her thighs, when she wears a bathing suit, you can see thin blue veins. Arion had tissue-thin skin like that. I once saw an octopus, hauled up on a dock, with skin so thin, pink and blue veins showed through. It was helpless, dying out of its watery world.

Were you afraid of dying away from home, my Arion? I dream of running, invisible, alongside you. I see myself in shadow and you, looking handsome in your army uniform, running across the battlefield. If you cry out for help I can't reach you. In my dreams I never touch you. I run with you across battle-scarred fields, jumping the mortar pocks, hearing the whine and sizz of flying bullets that leave their tracings on the night sky.

I'm invisible, without wings. We belly-squirm together under the barbed wire. The forgotten moon arcs overhead, effaced by the light of flares. It's all very exciting and only a little bit frightening, because I know I am there, your angel.

Over and over I dream, the same moon, our moon sailed over from Port Salish, the same war, night after night spent guarding you, racing at your side. I worry when I do not dream it.

Once I dreamed of you beside me calling for help in a nightmare; you in my bed in your khaki uniform and I afraid to reach out and touch you for fear of what it might mean outside the dream. And then I woke up and found myself fumbling for the light switch so that I could find you. . . .

Perhaps at that moment you were running for your life in the real war, squinting your eyes shut, hunching your body over, your long legs stumbling under you, dead soldiers all around you. That was the only question I never asked in my letters to you: "Are you afraid of dying, Uncle Arion?" I told you most things and asked nearly everything—but that. I even asked, *"Do you think about Gladys a lot?"* Of course you said you did. *"Are you going to get married and have children, little girls like me?"* I even asked if soldiers thought a lot about women, knowing how quickly a soldier could die . . . and did those soldiers think about unborn children too?

I can't ask Mom such questions; she would be em-

barrassed. I wouldn't even ask you those questions now.
Why did you stop writing?

I loved all your letters, but best of all when you
wrote about Bart from the prairies:

"Want to hear about Bart, Anna? Well I'll tell you: He's
a short stocky guy, muscular, with a slightly gimpy foot that
the medics let pass because he was a high-school track star.
He's got black hair, darkish skin, slanted eyes, and used to
have a beard, but had to shave it off for the army. He says
his mother's related to Genghis Khan—my guess is, half Indian. He's shy, but when his tongue's on fire his words flower
like bloomin' songbirds. Those four-letter words, which us
guys need like food itself, he gives more beauty than church
hymns. Wouldn't hurt a fly. Me and him are buddies like me
and Will was. He's a great guy. Bart's hometown is Portage
la Prairie—Flat Bush I call it, just kidding. He's shy, keeps his
tongue still when he's around women—and a good thing or
they'd mob him. We're buddies. Boy, what he could do with
women if he half tried. I been through good times and bad
with him. Lying in three-inch trenches, pinned flat to mother
earth, with the 'shells flying thick as starlings' as Bart says,
pounding so damn hard . . . so damn bloody thick, you can't
raise your head. Have to turn sideways to blow your nose
pinched in your fingers.

"I shouldn't be telling you this, you're just a little girl. But
who can I tell if I don't tell you, Anna? I can't tell Gladys, she'd
be too upset. And I can't upset the folks either. For them I
make out like I'm a tourist, world traveller visiting the Eiffel
Tower. I tell them the nice things, like the time Bart and I
made our trench our castle. We gathered wood, laid a floor,

built walls, a roof. Made that trench home, me and Bart from Flat Bush. He pasted the walls with photos of back home in all seasons, mile after mile of prairie summer grass, dusty roads, marching telephone poles, and snow. Most guys put up pinups. And they talk plain raw—but not about wives or steadies or sisters (or nieces, ha, ha), because they're sacred. Bart gets kidded a lot about his photo gallery. Homesick for his prairies is poor Bart. I just write nice things home, like about Bart and my castle—sure miss that castle—miss my home and you, Anna. Hope you don't mind, Anna, about the hard things I write you, my honey."

I get teary remembering "honey," and remembering what happened to silver-tongued Bart.

"Why, Anna, you're crying." It's Cousin Alice, smooth as vanilla pudding, come out again, smiling after being joshed about her baking a matrimonial cake. "What's the matter, Anna?"

"Nothing."

"Oh. Well all right dear, if you say so . . . Anything I can do, love?"

"It's fine, Alice," Ginny says from the doorway. "I think she just wants more time."

"Time? Oh? . . . I see. Well, I'll just go then. Godfrey is waiting for me at the gate."

They'll be married in only a few weeks. I know that he can't wait to be with her, and that she can't wait to be with him . . . they're lucky.

Homecoming Minus 4

I wrote him and wrote him.

A long time ago he answered: "Young men don't think much about unborn children." That's all he said. No, his exact words were: "Young men try not to think too much about unborn children."

To the right I see Gramps' foot propped up on his footstool; to the left I see the sweltering black-and-silver stove, with an armload of fresh cut pale-yellow fir and orange alder drying out under it. Kindling and dry logs fill the old woodbox Gramps built when he was a young man. Gran sweats over the stove; I can see one straight leg in its lisle stocking, her puffy ankle spilling over her flat-heeled slipper. I can only hear Gemma around the corner washing something in the sink.

Uncle Arion, I miss you so! It's more than a year 34 since you last wrote me. Why? I sit here in our spot all alone re-reading your letters. They all tell me, "Put those old letters away; why mope over old letters; we should burn those old letters."

Don't you feel sorry for me? Don't you miss me at all?

"I got to tell you about last Wednesday. I got to tell you about Bart, you little pigeon-toed dove. Last Wednesday we were lying in our scraped-out ruts keeping our heads down, noses pressed flat in the dirt. Bart and I were some fifteen yards apart shelling this German tank, just making pests of ourselves; it was too far off for us to be more than pesky. But I guess that tank kind of took offense, because it turned suddenly and came growling our way. It must have figured out where Bart was lying—I got up on one knee, saw him sunk down low as he could lie, his hands clasped over his helmet. Then the tank drove right on top of him—the guys dragged me down—and pivoted three times. I went crazy grappling with the five guys hanging on to me. When one of the guys, pressing down my shoulders, yells, "Hey look at that, will ya!" Bart pops up like a damn prairie gopher. I can see his lips moving, letting fly with a ream of fucking cuss words. Bart the poet. He takes careful aim—BAM—blows the bloody left tread right off that tank.

"Immobilizes it. You never saw a crew more thunder-struck than that tankload of swine when they crawled out, scared shitless, into the cross fire. A sight like that did our hearts good, I'll tell you, little girl. We felt like runnin' over and pounding Bart on the back, addin' to his bruises. But we were pinned flat as I say. It was risky just blinking. So we all just lay there hollerin', 'Yea! Yea, Bart, yea!' "

I always like the letters about Bart. He would have liked it here at Gran and Gramps', if Arion had brought him to visit us. I would have liked him . . . and he would have liked me; we could have talked and listened and been friends forever and ever. Maybe he could have married Ginny.

Maybe he could have married me.

Once I asked Uncle Arion, *"Did you choose to go to war?"*

He wrote back:

"I was thinking of it. I believed the government posters, 'Join the War and See the World'—but they forgot to add the last word, Anna. 'Join the War and See the World DIE.' Bart says that everyone was colored 'brave' in those posters, but they didn't color the blue ache of boredom and the blood-red taste of fear. Besides, everyone else was joining up."

And he sent me his favorite verse:

> "When I was standing in the street
> As quiet as could be,
> A great big ugly man came up
> And tied his horse to me.

"It's like that, Anna. I was a virgin when they tied this war on me.

"Did the fucking government ever tell us that everything sounds backward in war? That alone is enough to make you crap your pants. Did they ever say, 'In the war, soldier, when you hear the pop of the shot leaving the barrel, it's already too late? Soldier, the explosion is first and everybody blows up around you—and then there's the *zzzt* and then the pop as the shot leaves the barrel'? Did they ever tell us that!"

"Don't you ever ask why you are fighting?"

"Sure, we ask. But do we get any believable answer? No siree! It's mother-love, country, pumpkin pie, and baked beans. Fart, fart."

I sit and wait. I've got no choice.

"Halloo." Marsh waves from the back field. "Coming trapping?" I see the muskrat traps hung over his shoulder and know there is a lunch in his packsack. Boy trips around him in happy circles.

"No thanks!" I holler. He's headed for Rudy's Slough, my place of peace; I'm sorry not to be going.

I'll feel better when Aunt Cessy gets here. She's great. Arion likes her too.

It's getting hot, and I feel grumpy. Inside I hear them talking; talking behind my back; I lean . . . "Mutter mutter . . . Arion . . . whisper . . . something something . . . whisper . . . Arion." I keep hearing Arion's name. Their whispering annoys me. I can see straight through the hall. And in the dark at the end of the hall I can just make out the velvet drape hung to seclude the parlor. The parlor is not for family, it is the preserve of special guests, exotic jungle beasts who never seem to come calling. Gran and Gramps' bedroom is on the left. I know what's in there.

"Get off your *derrière*, and fetch Gramps a piece of his smelly cheese for *déjeuner*," Gran hollers to me.

"Yeah! And get some wood while you're at it," <u>37</u>

Gemma chimes in. "We're fresh out! You're a layabout, Anna; you'll get fatter yet!"

"I'm not fat," I yell.

"Don't worry, you will be."

I'm not moving. I'm waiting for my uncle. It would take a grenade to budge me.

"Don't bother her," Gramps says. He slumps back down in his chair, and after a little while he asks in a sleepy voice for the time, even though lunch is at exactly the same time every day.

Oh, well, I get up and go through to the pantry. I step sideways into the darkened bedroom where the curtains are always drawn, smelling the oiled floors and old cheese, listening to the heavy-handed ticktock of the alarm clock. One by one I look over all the pictures of Gran's sons and daughters, all my aunts and uncles, all grown now, and some dead. Mom is there looking shy, beside Aunt Lud who was still innocent in the days before diminutive Uncle Hud bulled his way into her life. The twins, Gemma and Ginny, are arm in arm. Gran sits poised motionless in her engagement picture all alone.

Arion told me how Gran, his mom, had snuck off from her seamstressing job in Flanders to marry Gramps who was considered a ne'er-do-well and headed for a bad end—and he was German besides. They married and left the old country, and Gran never did hear from her family again. Arion told me about it like it was just-one-of-those-things, the way boys see it. It's hard to feel sorry for Gran though, because if you do she acts insulted— but I sure do feel sorry thinking of how she's an old lady now who never heard from her mom and dad and her sister from the day she turned a young bride.

Gramps stands in a badly faded photo beside his favorite thoroughbred horse and sulky—in the days before he lost all his money.

Then I look at the photo, which I know as if it were my very own, of Uncle Arion dressed in uniform. The picture sits on his broken yellow chair.

I broke that chair. In a fit of temper. Looking at it, I'm ashamed. Uncle Arion would never have lost his temper and done what I did with that chair. I step back into the pantry and grab the cheese and hurry out to Gran.

"Here," Gran says, and she goes to the sewing drawer and gives me more toothpicks and buttons to go with the yellow potatoes, as my reward. I feel silly; I'm much too old for what Gemma calls my "Arion Zoo," but of course I take them anyway.

Out on the porch I make a potato dog Boy, covering it with his fur, then another potato soldier. I put Boy in Arion's lap. Not that Boy ever sat in Arion's lap. Everybody doesn't have to be an animal lover, I guess. But Arion should be grateful because Boy's given up swatches of fur to give him hair.

Then I find myself making a potato chair like the chair I broke when I was eleven. When Arion was already fighting in the war.

I sat facing the garden running my fingers along the rungs of Arion's yellow chair, sitting in this chair because it was my Arion's. I didn't see Marsh sneaking through the garden.

Marsh snuck through the flower bed, and then . . . HA! He popped up in front of the window, pressing his face into an ugly stranger's, flat on the glass. I nearly fell over backward off Arion's chair!

Marsh stuck two fingers in his ears and waggled the others at me. He stuck his tongue out. He thumbed his nose. "Acting like a brother," Dad calls it. So I ignored him—if that's the way he wanted to be, we just wouldn't be friends!

He pulled faces, thumbed his nose some more, and mouthed, "You and your Arion!"

I hated it whenever my brother acted ugly. What did I ever do to him! I tried to think of what Dad said at such times: "So he's jealous." Ha. "Why don't you spend more time with him."

Marsh jumped up and down, puckered up, and pointed at his backside, then at me.

I'd be nice if he'd be nice.

I turned on him. "Ass, ass," I hissed under my breath so Gran couldn't hear.

He gestured wildly. "Kiss my . . ."

Gran busily chopped up chives for potato salad. "Ass!"

Marsh stretched his mouth, shouted silently some more. I lip-read, "Arion's gone, he's gone—and he's not sorry either!" He waved and danced, sticking out his bum.

I picked up the yellow chair by its back and waved

it, threatening him. He danced around jerkily, pointing at his ass, stretching his mouth, staggering pigeon-toed, careful not to step on Gran's flowers. Then he looked up cross-eyed and wiggled his single-jointed thumb at me.

I crashed the chair through the window. The rungs broke off on the windowsill. The seat and legs flew into the garden. Uncle Arion's favorite chair.

Marsh lay on his back in the middle of the peonies, stunned—but not hurt.

The remains of Arion's chair were in my hands. My brother on his back in the garden. Shattered glass. Not a drop of blood spilled. I turned.

Gran stood, caught in mid-act, in the dark at the back of the kitchen. I stood in the spotlight before the broken window with the dust filtering through the sun's rays. The evidence was in my hands. The soup went on cooking, the stove throwing out heat into the hot kitchen. Silence, except for the clock ticking through the bedroom wall. Gran stood, a bowl of potato salad upside down on top of her bunioned feet.

I wonder if the moment you die is like that; you fight it and can't believe you're doing it.

Uncle Barnard heard about that chair and he was the one who told Mom on us. She took me aside and said I'd been foolish. I was so ashamed. Uncle Arion would never have done a thing like that no matter how mad he was.

I wrote him a letter that evening, saying I hoped he

wouldn't be mad at me. I hoped he would laugh—not at me; I didn't want him to laugh at me! He wrote:

" 'Proportion before contortion. It's only a chair.' That's what Bart says."

Once I got over how he told Bart, I thought, It's only a chair is right—and a broken window—and an enraged Gran—and an almost crippled brother—and a nasty-tempered brat, me. Oh, yes, and a ruined potato salad. I guess he laughed; I hope he laughed . . . and enjoyed himself for once—even if it means he laughed at me . . . with Bart.

But now, all that seems so unimportant. My potato Arions look foolish, leaning against each other and falling over.

Homecoming Minus 3
IN THE MORNING

When he comes, I'll have his potato presents ready.

Gramps is snoring. How can he sleep at a time like this? Marsh is off with his best friend Joe, and my best friend Sal Anne is out on her dad's gill-netter, cooking and keeping him company. And this summer I haven't done anything with my Gramps . . . except wait for Arion—and that's not "together," with Gramps in there on his chair and me out here on the steps. I hope he gets up soon and goes out walking like his old self. Maybe he will when Arion comes . . . if Arion comes. Maybe Aunt Cessy will drop by soon in one of her gaudy outfits and cheer him up some. Gramps isn't even telling his old fish stories anymore. Marsh says they're glorified lies. That was when I was just a kid and first started asking questions about Gramps. I wish I never had, 'cause of what Mom said.

I wrote Arion, *"Does Gramps lie?"*

I asked Ginny, "Does Gramps lie?"

"Your Gramps!" She laughed, pulling a funny face and shrugging.

"Dad, does Gramps lie?"

"Yep."

I couldn't ask Gran!

I was sorriest when I asked Mom.

"Mom, does Gramps really lie?" I asked her when I was only eleven.

"Your gramps, Anna? Well, he's not the man he once was." She had finished putting the wild roses I'd picked her into a jam jar. "He used to be different. He was something like Arion, young, tall . . . except that he was very rough with us. If at meals we put our elbows on the table, he'd grab our wrists and crack down hard." She winced.

My gramps!

"It wasn't so bad for us girls, but he was a hard man—hard on his horses and harder on his boys. Your gran was too busy with so many young tugging at her skirts—another always riding her apron high—to do much protecting in those days." Mom's hand was on my shoulder, but she seemed to have forgotten me; a reflection of her head floated balloonlike in the kitchen window. I was sorry I asked. "He beat a horse once"—she went on—"when it lost a race," she shuddered. Then she remembered me and half smiled. "Course it's different now, with grandchildren. He loves you—not that he didn't love us—but a man feels hard pressed with so many children—why, if they'd all lived, there would have been seventeen of us! Sometimes there was so little food . . . and he couldn't do much more than watch us hunger. We were the poorest in Skyburn, the poorest in the whole prairie. I used to think, 'poorest in the world.' Our shoes were passed down, they slopped on our feet or pinched. We carried them in our hands most of the way to school, not to wear them out. One year there were no shoes for me, so I quit. That was in grade five. Your aunt Lud got a pair of bloomers so full of holes she had to keep her legs together and stay right side up; it nearly killed her, but that's how she became a lady."

Aunt Lud a tomboy! Aunt Lud who always says, "Ladies never pick their noses or talk vulgar or grind their teeth or chase boys!" Aunt Lud who collects bone china and holds tea parties in a living room snowed under in a blizzard of doilies; Aunt Lud who says, "Excuse me!" *before* she farts! That Aunt Lud! "You mean our Aunt Lud was a tomboy once?"

Mom stood with a hand on her broad hip, her flowered dress wavy above her sturdy ankles, feet in proper walking shoes; she looked at me in my bare feet. "Yes, your aunt Lud."

"But what about Gramps?"

"Your Gramps?" Mom drifted off. "Well there was no point in our reproaching him . . . but we all did, in our turn, as we got older. . . . 'Awh, Dad, not another one!' When we were young we didn't comprehend. I remember, he used to tuck the shoe box under his arm each time and set out for town to register and bury . . . we 45 knew another baby had died . . . I remember, each time a shoe box—" Mom takes her hand off my shoulder. "Oh, Anna! There now, you're a sensible girl—put your shoes on. That's all in the past. You and Marsh, why you are your gramps' bloodline—his sunshine. It was foolish of me to tell you all this. You go play now."

Instead I had gone to visit Arion's girl friend, Gladys. "Hi, Gladys. My uncle Arion asked me to call on you," I told her.

"Oh, hi, did he, honey? Yes, well, I'm glad and all that but . . . ah . . . I smashed my thumb in the cash drawer. Yah, that's what happened, and so I haven't written lately."

"Who's the cute kid, Glady babe?" A short thin man with a crew cut and wearing a sailor's suit walked out of the back room. "Who's the cute toots?" He had a blue-red Capricorn tattooed on his right arm.

Gladys was all frilly in a white summer dress with a funny-looking black tassely shawl painted with pink roses, draped over her shoulders.

"Her? Oh, this is my beau's other girl," Gladys cackled. "I was just telling her how I smashed my finger in the cash drawer. Oh, ya, and this guy, this is my cousin Herb. You know . . . cousin?"

"Sure, I got cousins." I had nowhere else to look; I saw the sailor's left arm; it said "Cancer" underlined with a snake in blue and red. He spotted me staring at it; he flexed it, and the snake moved like it was alive.

"Want to see the equator?"

I looked away.

"Yes . . . ah . . . well you just send your uncle my love

and tell him I'll be writin' soon and you tell him all about how I smashed my thumb in the cash drawer and how it hurts and makes it hard for me to write—oh yeah, and I'll tell him myself when I write."

I looked at her thumb, and her fingers too, but there was nothing to see.

"It's why I ain't been writing, toots. You sure look cute, like the sailor says. Someday you'll grow up to look real nice."

"She looks terrific to me right now." The tattoo gave me a wiggle. "It's purity and innocence what does it." He blew me a kiss. "Sure you don't want to see the equator, honey bun?" He winked. Gladys gave him a black look, and he shrugged.

"Okay, baby, okay. It means nothing to me."

All I knew was if I were her and I'd lost my arms, both legs, and couldn't write with my toes, and was nothing but a trunk, then I'd have someone stick a pencil in my teeth like the seal man at the carnival or I'd peck at a typewriter with my nose until I was more cross-eyed than ever so I could write my Arion. I pictured her like that, a truncated body, cross-eyed, pecking with her nose—I liked that picture. But that was so ugly of me I said good-bye and ran right home and wrote Uncle Arion a cheery letter about how fine Gladys was except for her thumb and two fingers she'd caught in the cash drawer. And I told him how she'd be writing soon. I also told him how happy I had been that his yellow chair with its broken back was gone—but then I found it in the bedroom, beside the bed, as a nightstand. I should have known, nothing with a breath of life in it is ever thrown out around Gran's house. I swore in that letter, not because of the bloody chair but because of HER. I waited a long time for an answer. At last he wrote back:

"I don't mean to be tough on you, but, honey, please don't swear, it's not ladylike."

When I got back from Gladys', Marsh told me what had happened to Gramps.

From the distance it had looked as if the car had hit a paper bag; it blew up and seemed to spiral in the after rush of wind. Gramps saw it wasn't any paper bag. Gramps' cat, the one he had back then, Old Gray, ran in tighter and tighter circles, chasing the pain like a kitten after its tail, almost flying around and around on the spot until finally he collapsed.

The man in the car had looked back and then stepped on the gas, spraying gravel as he flew on down the road through the Reserve and out of sight.

Gramps started running toward Old Gray in his slow way. Marsh ran past him. Gray was lying, his mouth opening and shutting. "Reflexes, son, that's all; reflexes." Gramps squatted beside the small body and ran his lumpy fingers through his own thin hair. Gray stopped twitching finally, and he picked him up. "Go home, Marsh, go home, son. Get the shovel."

I couldn't believe it about Gramps being hard on his horses, beating them . . . hard on his boys, beating them. And yet I certainly couldn't not believe it when it was Mom who told me.

❋   ❋   ❋

I pick out the silliest, ugliest looking potato I can find and begin to work on a Gladys.

" 'Lo, Anna." Gramps has his cap on. "Coming for a stroll by the river?"

I feel so sorry for Gramps, a young man once, full of promise, hard on his horses and his boys, having to court his sons, seeking forgiveness for being a father.

"Oh, Gramps." I hug his old bent legs; he's still my Gramps. "I'd love to, Gramps, but . . ."

"That's all right, my child." He pats me. "I understand. You look after your Arion . . . he needs you now more than I, God knows . . . and He's probably looking in the opposite direction. Better not let your gran hear that bit of blaspheme," he says extra loud so Gran will hear.

Arion wrote:

> "If you laugh you lie.
> If you cry, you die."

I wonder if he was quoting Bart?

> "P.S. Gramps was hard, but easier on me, I was among the last, remember, a family baby. It's okay. Your gramps loves you, and he loves me too, I guess. Not to worry, Anna."

It made me cry to think of Gramps beating his sons and then, before he could make it better between Arion and him, getting that telegram from the war office.

At least I still have my letters:

"I lie on my cot, Anna, my arms folded under my head ('like angel wings,' Bart says) and stare at the light bulb, or at my bayonet propped against the far wall. Bart lies on his stomach like always. If it weren't for Bart, Anna, I don't know. I just don't know. Lordy, is that man entertaining. Funny! Last night he told us the tale of his sex life. I rolled right off my cot onto the floor. 'I heard a lot of talk about sex,' he said. 'So I thought I'd just try it. Well I found this girl who felt the same way. So we tried it. Jesus God, what a wretch! What a mistake!' The guys were all grinning. 'Hell, we swore we'd never do it again!' The guys are all tittering. 'Then we noticed everybody was getting married. So we did that too. It was okay at first, but after a bit we noticed our friends all had these babies crawling around. Someone told us, "That's how you do it." So we did it again. Lordy, we'd forgotten—the pain—the misery—the HUMILIATION!' Some of the guys get cramps from laughing, holding on to their guts like they've been bayoneted. I lie on the floor howling and crying. One Frenchie from Montreal is dancing around cuppin' his crotch and yelling, 'Wooooo wee woooeeee, he got ta be an Englishman from way out west, zat one, woo ee. He got ta be a *maudit Anglais* from ze prairie!' Bart lies there on his stomach, poker-faced. 'I'm from Portage la Prairie,' he says. The Frenchie rolls his eyes, 'Yah, Flat Bush, wooo eeeee.' Bart lies there waiting for the Frenchie to cool, then he goes on, 'Our son was eight years old when he said he wanted a sister. So, my wife and I, we did it again. Guess we'd forgotten. Lord God, the agony of it burned in our memory that time, I can tell you! By God, we learned our lesson that time!' 'Wooooooo eeeee.' The guys are grinning at the two of them —Bart and the Frenchie. 'Never again. Never again!' That guy

Bart, he's everything. Who am I? I'm nothing. But that guy Bart he's something else. Then this Frenchie sobered up suddenly, like soldiers will. 'It's hard ta sleep alone when you're an old married man like me. I just pray ta God I can go back ta my old woman for some of zat pain.' "

That letter confused me. I thought sex was supposed to be fun—especially for men.

Our poor Arion. His luck turned bad: First there was the war, and then, a little while after he left us, his luck took a real nose dive, thanks to Gladys. As it happened, I found out before he did.

I cried. I cried and slept with that letter so now it's all stained and crumpled. I'm crying now, as I stick pins in potato Gladys.

Gramps returns from his river walk, looking lost. I hide porcupine Gladys behind my back and look away as he passes. Did he notice?

"What's up, girl?" Ginny is right behind him. She taps me lightly on the head and vanishes into the kitchen.

Will I ever be sixteen like the twins? Uncle Arion loves his sister, Aunt Ginny; he's like her, carefree. He loathes his other sister, Aunt Gemma; he's a lot like her too. We're all a bit like each other, and I guess that only makes sense; we're family.

These crazy tears streaming down my face! I'm hoping no one else comes.

"Anna Swales!" Gemma yells. "That you blubbering?"

Cuss it, did Ginny tell? No, of course not. I start in humming. It starts out "Teddy Bears Picnic" and comes 51 out Uncle Arion's favorite verse, skipping through my head and humming out my nose:

> When I was standing in the street
> As quiet as could be,
> A great big ugly man came up
> And tied his horse to me.

Arion claims that one was written special for him:

"It was like that for me. I was just growing up in Port Salish, on the streets and in the fields and along the riverbank, just a-floating on the summer river like nature intended, when all of a sudden up comes war and ties this big one-eyed horse he calls Death to me pretty bod."

Marsh comes up. "You look . . . strange . . . sitting here all the time." Marsh sits down on the far side of Boy, who thumps up a regular cloud of dust in his happiness and leans against Marsh and slobbers and dribbles his love on his jeans. Boy likes my brother a lot . . . which is understandable . . . after all, Boy is his dog too. And I like Marsh. I guess I even love him. I actually feel a little better now that he's here.

We stare out over the greengage plum trees, the field, and the fence to the glassy river. All this, the earth, was here before we were born; dinosaurs browsed in our valley, on the flats and on the riverbanks; prehistoric fish swam in the inlets and in the lakes; maybe pterodactyls winged over our mountains and screamed across our landscape before they finally became extinct. And in a flood I think of all those I love. I'm glad Dad didn't make it into the war because of his chameleon eyes. I'm glad for me and my brother that he didn't. And I'm glad for him. I miss Arion, who made it. I asked, *"Did you ever think of the enemy as fathers and sons, as husbands and brothers, Arion?"*

"Sure."

"Did you ever think of some of those enemy soldiers being sort of like yourself? Did you ever think of that?"

"Yeah. And then we killed them. Once we wiped out a whole battalion of fourteen-year-olds. They wouldn't give up, you see."

"Weren't you sorry, terribly terribly sorry?"

"This is war, Anna."

"You should be happy," Marsh says sadly. "Arion is coming home."

I can't seem to make much of even Marsh's company these days. We used to keep each other such plain good company; he loves Arion too.

"I said, you should be happy." Marsh jostles me.

"Why happy?"

"Why not? No matter what, Uncle Arion's coming home, isn't he? So you could at least try and act happier."

"Something tells me . . . it's not going to be happy . . . this homecoming."

"Hmmmmph. Just maybe he needs you to act happy."

"What do you mean?"

He growls, "I'm being happy; otherways he might never come home at all." He looks to the field, scowling.   <u>53</u>

What does he mean? He sure isn't fooling me with his "happiness."

Gramps' Manx cat walks up out of the tall grass and past us, ignoring us. Gramps' other cat, Old Gray, had been friendly at least. Ungrateful beast, this Manx.

Gramps pinches Gran's arm as she sails by; I think of how she likes the color blue and wonder if she likes the tiny blue bruises he makes on her body.

"Non, vieux! You're an old fool!" She clacks her false teeth.

It used to make me angry at Gramps. When I was little, he used to threaten me. "I'm going to trade your gran in at the five-and-ten-cent store." Now it just makes me sad.

Marsh has moved along the step and is looking away from me. "Wonder how Arion is?" I say.

"Arion?" He rubs the back of a hand. "Yeah." Marsh isn't exactly talkative.

Gran whips by, too close to Gramps, and he pinches her backside. Maybe Gran likes Gramps to pinch her— and that makes me feel even sadder. I look at Marsh again. "I've overheard . . . things."

Marsh clenches his fists. "Oh, yeah?" His thumbs are tucked in. He's bent forward and his face is hidden under his black forelock—I can just see how he's biting his lip. I feel sorry for him. "What things?"

". . . Nothing really."

"Well, Sis, the truth—only as I figure it—is . . . maybe I should—"

"I know it's nothing, Marsh!"

"I don't know for sure, Sis, but—"

"He's my favorite uncle!"

"Yeah." He sits up straight. "Right. It's only what I figured on my own anyway, and I guess it'll work out somehow. You'll see, most likely your favorite uncle is going to remember. He'll most likely spot you first off . . . sitting right here in your old . . . He'll probably rush right up and grab you and throw you up in the air, the way he always used to do . . . or something. . . ."

I blush. We both blush. Such a gush of words isn't like Marsh. I know how much he wants this to happen for me.

"Uncle Arion, how could you kill other people's brothers and fathers with families waiting at home just like we wait for you! How can you do that!" I was sorry as soon as the letter hit the bottom of the mailbox.

"Easily, Anna. You see your buddy shot . . ."

Oh, no. Not Bart!

". . . writhing, wounded on the ground. Bart from Portage la Prairie."

Oh no, oh no, not Bart.

"I didn't want to tell you. You watch some bloody German, some damn Kraut, casually toss a grenade between Bart's legs. Bart from Flat Bush. You think you don't care! You care all right. You hurt. Bart. Bart told me that he wasn't going to make it out of this war. 'I'm not going home, Arion old buddy,' he said. 'I'm not going to howl no more.' I thought it was just despair talkin', because that morning while I was quaffing a drink at the water truck this guy standing next to 55

Bart got shot without hardly a sound. They were standing under a maple tree, much like the trees back home, when this guy looks down at his chest and says, 'My God, I've been shot!' and falls down dead with a tiny hole in his breast pocket turning red around the edges. Sniper fire. I told him, 'Nah, Bart, you're immortal.' But I watched out for him after that. 'Before this war is done, I'll be sleeping on my back, Arion.' Then, one afternoon, I lost sight of him for just a minute or so . . . most guys think their numbers will never come up . . . I turned, but I was too late—only just in time to see it happen. I froze for a second—then I ran for him—there was this Kraut standing over him, grinning with his bayonet red and Bart's eyes wide in surprise and his mouth openin' and shuttin'—I never made it—one of our guys brought me down with a tackle . . . only six inches from where I turned to run. I saw Bart fall and the Kraut, walking backward, roll this grenade between Bart's legs, aimin' for the crotch. Bart couldn't have noticed, he was too busy with both hands trying to stuff his intestines back inside himself. It happened so fast I saw the grenade blow as I was falling, I swore Bart was screaming! . . . long after he was dead—it was me screaming. Jesus, Anna. I guess I loved that man."

IN THE AFTERNOON

I place my potato Bart in a huge match-box coffin.
Gran, with an old pair of socks in her hand, bustles

into the pantry. "Some things just can't be mended, *vieil homme.*"

A potato Arion kneels beside Bart's coffin.

Gramps leans way over and looks after her into the hall. "Hey Maw, they're my favorite pair of socks."

"They're all your favorite once they're worn out." She tucks them in the rag bag and comes out carrying a plate of cheese at chest height.

"Oui, oui, ma chérie," Gramps says, teasing her in French and giving her a big blue pinch as she swings past.

"Vieux fou!" Gran squawks. "Old fool!"

He chuckles and goes to work with a razor blade on his corns.

Gran's making cottage cheese, and she sends Gemma outside with a cheesecloth bag of curds and whey to hang for dripping under the loganberry trellis. I stick my tongue out at Gemma. She ignores that, stops, and stands with her hands on her hips for a moment. "You expect nothing to change! You think that just because you wish—"

"Gemma, come here!" Gran snaps.

What does Gemma know of what I think? Gemma doesn't ever know how I feel.

Two days to go. I've made today last a long time, but tomorrow will pass, then it will be only one day. And then none.

I roll onto one hip and pull out a letter. And just my luck, it's *that* letter, and Gemma comes tiptoeing up from my other side and before I can react, grabs it.

"Give that back!"

"What are you doing sitting here, Anna? It looks dumb."

"Nothing."

"What's the matter, girl?"

Everything—everything's the matter—but right now the worst is that she's got my letter. "Nothing's the matter. Give me back my letter!"

She takes the liberty of sitting beside me, then starts in reading my letter out loud: "'. . . young men don't think . . .'" She looks smug, holding the letter at arm's height so I have to strain for it. She tilts over sideways with me on top of her. "'. . . unborn babies . . .'" She reddens. "'. . . They wouldn't get very far if they stopped to worry about . . .'" She sucks her teeth, just like Gran, holding my letter way out at arm's length. Serves her right, I pray that someday she learns every ugly truth on earth and in hell. "Typical! of a man!"

"It is not. It is not typical of a man." I crawl over her, trying to get my letter back. "I bet some men think about unborn babies. I bet some men think about unborn babies a whole lot."

"But not your perfect uncle Arion, eh! Not your glorious M-A-N!" She's flat on her back. I'm on top of her, but she has me there. I push myself up, digging an elbow into her budding breast. She groans but doesn't admit to owning breasts. She sits up and dusts herself off, frowning, and plucks slivers out of her elbow. She combs her precious mud-brown hair with her pomegranate fingernails. "Such intimate questions you ask, Anna. It wouldn't hurt you or Arion to think a little more about God and His divine order."

What's that supposed to mean? "At least I don't go around grabbing other people's mail, Miss Self-righteous." I snatch up my letter.

"You'll marry a strange man, Anna, mark my words!"

What does she know? My man is going to be pure—a brain, not a body—a genius, who'll live in a log cabin in the woods and love children. What does she know about a man like that!

I hate Gemma; I'll never forgive her for what she did to me and my gift from Uncle Arion. That was a couple of months after my twelfth birthday, when I received the toy dishes from Arion. My Arion who hadn't written in so long.

I was lying on the twins' bed in their attic bedroom, watching Gemma and Ginny brush their hair, and studying the water blisters and the bird-and-flower pattern on the wallpaper: lovebirds . . . or hummingbirds really . . . honeysuckle and morning glories. I turned my head past the open closet with the sprung hinge, the wardrobe with the blemished mirror, to the beauty of my twin aunts.

"Ninety-six . . . Don't stare, Anna, and stop counting . . . ninety-seven," Gemma snapped.

"Eighty-two, seventy-one," I muttered, as Gemma

stood at the dresser, brushed her hair the last stroke, unblinking, studying her reflection.

"One hundred one."

I watched my twin aunts to see what tips I could pick up on becoming a woman.

Ginny sat cross-legged on the mussed bed, and smiling, brushed her hair one hundred strokes; Gemma brushed one extra. Gemma's like that. She had to be born first—Ginny slid out easily seven minutes later! That was our Ginny. Gemma was serious and religious; life for her was a grind.

"Leave her be, Gemma, Anna's a pet." Ginny unfolded, stepped out into the middle of the room. It was only in the middle of the attic that they could stand upright. I could stand straight almost to the wall. She grinned at me as she lifted a long leg high, touching perfume behind her knee (lily of the valley), and then lifted the other leg high, and then perfumed the crook of her elbows, the spot behind each ear, the hollows at the base of her long neck, the cleft between her small narrow breasts. The perfume floated out the small stained-glass window, tulips and bluebirds.

Uncle Arion was going to be surprised when he came home; his sisters were just girls when he left them. He used to call them giraffes.

"Anna's a pet, a pet, a pet." Ginny blew me kisses.

"Anna a pet? That kid!" Gemma scowled. "A pest is more like it. She's always hanging around spying— more like a pet vulture!" Gemma plopped her foot beside me on the bed and started painting her toenails 60 (Pink Melon), without looking at me.

Ginny climbed onto the foot of the metal double bed and perched there. "I'm a vulture," she said. I snickered, and Ginny sneered, "I want MEAT! To hell with waiting—I think I'll murder my sister." She leapt at Gemma. I rolled aside and Gemma leaped backward. Ginny fluttered around on the creaking unmade bed.

Gemma groaned, "Now look! You mussed my polish." She stared at her big toe, and I rolled around in the bedclothes, snorting.

Ginny tickled me.

Ginny looked so pretty. I hated to say it, but Gemma did too. I could hardly wait to be like Ginny. I curled up in the warm hollow in the center of the bed, covered myself with the sheet, and felt my own breasts that Aunt Lud called "budding." (Uncle Hud always called me a heifer.)

"I'm off," Ginny said, twirling in the middle of the room like a ballerina and slipping on the worn linoleum like a drunk. "Off ta wrassel witch da evil demon lusht!"

"Oh, Ginny, you're so foolish!" But Gemma couldn't quite hide a smile.

Ginny bounced off down the stairs, me following . . . "You and I, Anna," she said, stepping in the worn hollows in the middle of the treads, "must have a serious talk". . . we bounded through the cold parlor . . ."sometime when I have" . . . and wafted into the warm kitchen where her beau was waiting . . ."more time."

He stood there, a dapper, natty French Canadian, city-pale, with a tiny mustache twitching and nostrils flaring at our Ginny, just like one of Uncle Hud's stallions nickering at its mare. I liked him.

It was sort of embarrassing. But then he waggled his ears at me, "Hi, *la princesse*." I wished he wouldn't call me that; I'm not his to call that.

It was fun to watch him work on Gran. He wheedled and flattered; she bristled, shook her finger at him—but she giggled. It was such an odd thing to see my gran giggle; she would never let me giggle. She shook her finger at him. He grinned. "Dance with me, Queen Bee." He grasped her shaking finger and wrapped an arm around her waist and waltzed her around and around the kitchen.

Arion used to dance her around the kitchen, down the hall and into the sacred parlor. She must have been thinking of him as she waltzed. Arion was the blazing sun for her; next to him, pale Frenchie was the moon eclipsed.

Ginny danced by herself, twirling across the checkered black-and-white linoleum. Gemma watched, disapproving and jealous, looking like the Good Christian.

I'd call her that too—if she was good to me.

Ginny kissed Gramps on top of his silver head and tripped off with her beau; Gramps blinked a couple of times, smiled after her, then dozed off again. Gran popped a pot roast in the oven, all the while whistling and twittering like a canary. It was a normal, everyday sort of day.

"Gran, can I have some bread dough for the little loaf pan Arion sent me?" I went to the bottom drawer of the big pine cabinet Gramps had built as Gran always said "with his own hands." I took out a box and opened

my two-week-old present; Uncle Arion's gift of baking

dishes suitable for a nine-year-old. At first I'd been insulted . . . today I know that I didn't really care. I hadn't heard from him in so long, I was just happy he'd thought of me at all. Were my dishes all the way from the front line?

Gemma chimed in, "What's the baby *enfant* up to now?"

I blushed. Silly dishes really. I patted the small loaf into its pan.

"Baking its itsy bitsy bread in its teeny weeny dishes?"

I hated her. I thought of hiding the dishes back in the dark cupboard, of giving them away.

Gran frowned at Gemma's painted toenails as Gemma scrubbed the little yellow potatoes for supper.

I didn't care. Arion loved me. He didn't send Gemma a gift, or Gladys. He sent me a gift. I put my little loaf on a stool a ways from the stove and laid a clean towel and Gran's old sweater over it to make it rise. I went and sat at the table.

After a while I got up and slipped the little loaf into the oven.

Aunt Gemma's beau tapped on the door. He was nothing special—just a couple of arms, couple of legs, a body, a head, and no tie or suit. It was as if courting Gemma was not enough of an occasion for him to dress up. I could see his point.

They settled on the bench behind the kitchen table. I sat down on Gramps' footstool; he was still sleeping, his knees drawn up. I hunched over and peeked from under his legs at the courting couple. It was fun. The beau tickled the soft underside of Gemma's arm, and she flushed, catching sight of me.

"Mom! Will you keep this child busy."

Child! Child, indeed, I was twelve years and two months. I huffed off.

I checked on my loaf. Almost done.

For something to do until I could safely sneak back and spy on Gemma, I lined my toy dishes along the counter top. I waited until everyone had forgotten me and then slipped back to Gramps' footstool. I held on to Gramps' foot, careful not to wake him, and watched the courting going on. The beau had put his hand on Gemma's knee under the table. I could see it beautifully.

Then she saw me. Gemma was always suspicious. She glowered at me.

"Let's go for a walk along the river," she said to him, spoiling my fun. I watched them till they were halfway down the path and I heard the gate slap shut.

When they were gone, for something to do that Gemma wouldn't like, I snuck upstairs to her bedroom and fooled around with the jars of creams and the lipsticks on her frilly dresser. But I soon got bored and so I strolled around upstairs until I was in front of Arion's old bedroom. I opened the door.

The room was bare, the way he liked it, stark, like an army barracks. There was a hard gray wool blanket for a bedspread on the metal bed. The curtain blew; the window was open to air the room. It had all been dusted, and on top of his egg-collection cabinet with its velvet drawers was a bouquet of straw flowers. I bet Ginny put it there.

I opened the closet and the moth-ball smell hit me. I wished I hadn't opened it. His graduation suit hung to one side, with tissue wrapped over the shoulders. A couple of pairs of dress pants. A pair of favorite jeans. A couple of shirts. On the floor his shoes were lined up. I didn't want to see any more. So I shut the door and went downstairs to wait for the lovers.

I didn't have to wait long. Gemma came walking up the path, looking sour. The boyfriend was half laughing, waving his hands in the air. He might have been trying to tell her a joke. Nobody could kill a joke like Gemma with her frown. He was trying to hold her hand, but she shook him off when she saw me spying. When they walked in through the open door, I strolled nonchalantly over to my baking set like I never had given it a thought while they were gone.

"Ha. Ha, ha," Gemma laughed at his joke.

The boyfriend gave a little groan. I sniggered. And I picked up my toy cookie sheet and studied it innocently, turning it around and around, sniggering. "What a dull day, full of ordinary people," I said.

"You said that before, you brat."

I turned, looking, and my elbow caught the casserole dish and *it* caught the pie plate and the pie plate caught the custard cups. They all crashed to the floor and shattered. I grabbed too late to save any pieces.

Gemma snorted, "Serves you right."

I couldn't believe it, all my dishes from Arion . . . smashed. My wonderful dishes . . .

Gemma snarled, "You don't think Arion just now sent you those dishes?"

"What do you mean?"

"Gran's had them stored away for ages and ages."

I looked at Gran. "How could you, Gran?"

Gran looked sorry; I was so mad I didn't care.

"You had too many, too many gifts for your birthday. What would you get later? I wanted for you to be happy . . . later . . . when you need happiness . . . not just *pour ton anniversaire.*"

She had made a fool of me. And now all my dishes were broken too. I struggled not to cry.

"They're only toys," Gemma said. "You're too old for them anyway, Anna."

"Who says so? God? You're mean, Gemma. You're the Devil!"

Her beau gave her a hard stare and knelt down to help me pick up the pieces. I cried loudly, I heard myself, gulping for air. Then Gran got out the dustpan.

I cut my finger, dropped the piece, but I didn't care, bleeding and sobbing. "I want my uncle Arion. I want my uncle Arion." I couldn't stop hiccuping.

Gramps woke up. *"Was ist das?"*

"Silly girl," Gemma said.

Smoke poured out of the oven where my loaf was burning.

"Gemma, don't be unkind," her boyfriend said.

Gran clucked, "Husha, husha."

I howled and howled.

A whiff of Limburger cheese from Gran's pantry hit us as the door slammed shut, and we heard Gemma pounding on up the stairs to the bedroom. Her beau picked up bits of glass, and Gran wiped up my blood.

Gemma's date was ruined. I was glad, glad, GLAD—
bawling and choking.

I still haven't forgotten. And haven't forgotten how
once Gemma yelled at Arion, "You're too darn charming
for your own good." That's silly. I thought for a moment
that he was going to hit her, but he turned and walked
away, keeping the peace.

I can picture all that in the past. What I can't really
picture is Uncle Arion home with us and everything like
it used to be.

"I smuggled this letter out past the authorities, the bastards. Last Sunday we got our own back, Anna, our pound of
flesh, our eye for an eye. If Bart has to sleep on his back it
seems only fair that six Krauts should lie on their backsides
forever. So I arranged it, me and a friend of Bart's. We got
orders to march a string of prisoners to the nearest transport,
some six miles off. That was the point for pick up and delivery
to the prisoner-of-war cages. Well we got back to camp inside of twenty minutes—delivery complete! No questions
asked. That kind of thing happens on both sides. But killing
the bastards didn't help. They didn't waste any love on us for
what we did to them and their buddies, Anna. But you're a
child, girl, and I shouldn't be telling a child such things, me,
a grown man. But I'll tell you, Anna, just you. When we shot
them it felt good. We made them watch us do it, one by one,
and then we rolled them over on their backs. But afterwards
it didn't feel good. And now it doesn't feel good at all. Goddamn it, Anna. I'm so frightened. I'm so goddamned fright-

ened most of the time now that Bart is, Jesus, I guess, GONE. And I have to tell somebody, and Jesus you're only a child to me. It doesn't make me feel good at all. And you never, never forget, Anna. I'm so goddamned frightened of the man I've become."

Will I never stop crying?

"I'm afraid of myself, Anna. And there's no fear worse."

And then I got the strange letter:

"I lie on my cot, Anna, arms folded, angel wings. I stare at Death, his teeth, his tails, his bat wings. Bayonet your brother. If ever the killer comes back home, I'll jump, my little dove, let us jump. I will, every time a door slams. I'll shoot myself in mirrors. Men with a few beers under their belts will make sport of me. Awh, Anna, my homely dove, my pouter pigeon, is that life for me? Stumble into the maw. Bart has left me his tongue."

What did it mean? What did it mean! I wrote him in a panic, *"What are you talking about, Uncle Arion! It's okay. You won't die. It's really okay to kill. It's okay by both sides, remember."* But that sounded crazy even as I wrote it.

I wished he'd never killed. Even if it meant he ran. When he comes home, I won't ask him.

Homecoming Minus 2

"Halloooo."

Aunt Cessy comes hallooing in the gate. She's alone as usual since Uncle Jerry is out fishing. She calls herself the out-law instead of the in-law. Her lips are red Cupid's bows, her nails have flecks of gold. She comes bombing along past the poplar sentinels, swinging her butt, past the loganberry trellis with its eternal bag of curds, singing along under the transparent apple tree. I know that if she met Gramps on the road, she'll have thrown him a kiss—or a bump and grind.

I want to run to her. But I sit still. A vigil is a vigil.

"How's my indi-vigil," asks Aunt Cessy, like reading my mind, "—and all her potatoes?"

Boy jumps straight up to her top-heavy chest and lands in a dust cloud at her feet, without once touching **69** her. He knows how quick she'd be to swat him! He rolls over.

"Damn dog!" She bends to scratch his belly. She's wearing short shorts, and from the back I know you can see two new moons of white flesh.

"Moon-bottoms," Gramps always mouths behind her, just to tease Gran. (Up front it's "balloons.")

Aunt Cessy stands, hands on hips, looking down at me. She's wearing her fried-eggs sweat shirt; the eggs too stare at me. She is very solemn. I'm enjoying the picture of me, loyal girl, sitting out the vigil, protecting the soldier off at war. Protecting a grown man?

"I see," says Aunt Cessy. "So that's how it is," mind reading, frowning. "Well the best of luck, my dear," and she goes inside to see what she can do to help Gran.

Suddenly Boy's ears lift, his tail beats up storm clouds, he leans forward, following his eyes out across the field. Marsh waves from the fence, and Boy is off like a shot. Some loyal dog! Traitor!

Marsh signals for me to come along gaffing. Boy crawls under the wire at his feet, but Marsh orders him to go back to me. Boy slinks my way. I wave, waving him free. Then I shake my head at Marsh, "Not coming," and sit back down and start adding up all the reasons I have to feel sorry for myself.

I'd love to be going, fighting salmon while they are still a bit lively, flashing silver. And then I'm up and running, smushing apples underfoot, careening out the gate. I get there all out of breath and just in time to shove Marsh and Boy off in the skiff.

"Hey Sis, why won't you come . . . please."

I stop, shake my head, I want to go—but. . . .

When I plop down on the steps once more, Gramps chuckles in his corner. "Glad to see you up, girl. Plenty of time to sleep when you're dead. By the way, what time is it?"

"Time for the salmon run, Gramps." I giggle.

We both laugh; that's the most indefinite time he's ever been given. We always laugh at each other's jokes, Gramps and I.

I watch Marsh and Boy until the skiff clears the bend. Beneath them the salmon will be swimming, silver, red, and spotted white with rot, struggling up river. Some will die—but not all.

"I'm rotten, Anna. I try. I try so damn hard, Anna, but I'm no darn good."

Cessy leaves. "Bye, love."

"Bye."

Gran and Gramps are whispering, crisscrossing languages. I lean backward and see Gramps standing close to Gran. Surprisingly, Gran is talking some German.

"What right to take my son . . . *mein guter Sohn* Arion . . . we work hard to bring him up right . . . manhood . . . Arion."

Gramps makes soothing sounds in French, "Hush a-hush a . . . *mais oui*, they took many boys, not only ours."

Gran snaps, "That makes it better? You can shrug and say, *'C'est la vie,'* eh?"

71

"*Non, non—Krieg ist Morden.* War is murder."

The water running in the sink makes it hard to hear. I block my ears, close my eyes . . . Arion, Arion, Arion . . . All I ask is that you stay the same. Is that too much?

"Oh God, Anna. Oh God, oh God oh my God."

Just be the same as when you first left us? Please.

When Uncle Arion comes home he'll be wrapped up in relatives' arms like a gift in ribbons. And mine. My arms will be around his neck as soon as he reaches the porch and swings me up, lifting me high above his army cap and letting me down gently and pressing me against his scratchy khaki wool soldier's uniform and holding me to his cold medals, and I'll trace over his epaulets and insignias with my finger and his fuzzy hair will shine in its halo from under his cap and his cheek will be warm against mine and his eyes blue as distant mountains. And I'll laugh till I'm hysterical and Gran will say "shush." And everything will be exactly as it was before. And after a bit I will release him for the others to hug.

I hope.

I feel myself float, like a feather.

It was more than four years ago that the first white feather arrived—that was before Arion went to war. I was with Gramps when he opened the envelope. He blanched and dropped the feather, which fluttered to the ground. "What is it, Gramps?" He didn't answer, he never spoke of it to anyone, not even Gran, I know that now. Of course, I told Arion. I shouldn't have, I know that now too. He blinked and went white. Two years later the second feather came. That was long after Arion had left.

"Another *weisse Feder*!" Gramps clutched it.

"A white feather!" Gran asked, "But why *une plume blanche*?"

By then I already knew what a white feather meant. So did Gramps. It meant you were a coward for not joining up to fight in the war.

"Mais non!" Gran cried. "You are too old, *vieil homme*, to go to war!"

"It is not for me. It is for Arion."

"But no! It cannot be. *Il est dans la guerre!*" Tears sprang into Gran's shoe-button eyes, and Gramps groaned.

"He is in the war," Gramps repeated. Gramps looked wounded, he muttered, *"Ja, ja, unser Junge*, our boy, is in the war, so why now do they send us *diese Feder?"*

They leaned together and held one another. I looked away out the window and heard Gramps choke down his sobs.

A dot and a smaller bouncing dot, that is all I can make out now of Marsh and Boy walking along the dam across the flats, headed for the waterline and ignoring the best gaffing spots. Marsh must be getting very lonely this summer, now his best friend Joe is gone again. And he hasn't got me anymore.

I spread all Arion's old letters out in a fan around me. It's plain to see how crazy the last ones are. I guess I've known that for some time now. Uncle Arion is crazy. No, I won't believe it.

I hear, way off across the field, a cow bell, beyond the mud flats, reminding me of Uncle Arion's letter:

"I hear cow bells across fields. They do not make me think of home. Of hell. Cold, hold, cold, hold. Hold me, child."

I blame a lot of it on his girl friend Gladys. He found out about her, and his letters lost heart.

"Hello, Anna dear." It's Aunt Lud from way over in the Fraser Valley. I stand up and hug her and see Uncle Hud out of one eye. I'd forgotten how she smells of fields of hay and Uncle Hud and cologne. She's so tall I only reach to her chest, which is no pillow. I feel bones. Good bony, gaunt old Aunt Lud dressed with frills like one of the valentines she's saved in her girlhood scrapbook . . . along with ticket stubs . . . faded corsages—not from Uncle Hud. Says Uncle Hud, "Chased me, your aunt did." Aunt Lud pouts, "Did not."

"My what a nice hug. And my haven't we grown!" she trills. "And so many pretty figurines. But potatoes! You should model in china clay, or at least, modeling paste."

She acts like I'm still a child in Pook's Hill Elementary—but I don't mind, seeing how it's her. She's always cheery. Uncle Hud says, "Your aunt Lud, she counts her chickens before they're so much as laid. Chose to marry me, she did."

"Did not."

Gran steps out on the porch to greet them. Uncle Hud stomps his tiny feet and shakes hands with Gran. He has the cow smell of the farm, not warm and milky like Aunt Lud, but rank and sharp like extra lemon in lemonade. Aunt Lud says, "Your uncle Hud, he's always whistling." (Maybe so, but he's not always whistling nice.) He calls her his old milk cow and me his heifer. "I chased her," he says, "till I tripped over her." He flexes a hand upside down, like a spider on its back. Aunt Lud snorts.

I've a plate of lunch in my lap, and Aunt Lud says, "A picnic on the porch with all your little potato friends, how nice." (Our aunt Lud, who'd say in the eye of a hurricane, "You see, I told you it was going to be a lovely day.") "But that man in the box . . . is that really nice, Anna?" she asks.

Uncle Hud gives her a tug, but she leans backward.

"And those battle scenes, Anna! How could you carve those faces? It's all too gory for a lady." She floats off in full sail.

Uncle Hud gives me a prod, "How's the heifer?" and follows his woman inside, rubbing his bullet head.

He always calls me a heifer. Aunt Ginny calls him the "basic man." Once I pointed out a fly on the porridge already in his spoon. Aunt Lud said, "Hush, Anna, that's bad manners to mention it." "But if I didn't, he'd eat it!" Uncle Hud winked at me and ate it.

"They are so opposite," Aunt Cessy once muttered. "How like great magnets they must meet in the night." It surprised me to hear Aunt Cessy sounding like a poet.

I can hear Aunt Lud making conversation. "The kitchen looks cheery," she says.

The kitchen is exactly the same as the day Aunt Lud's blind baby eyes first focused on it; from cave days and on, it's always been dark. Gran saves electricity; I remember when she used to snuff candles. Gran's a great snuffer, and Gemma's her disciple.

Gramps and Ginny, on the other hand, love light, and they sit as close to the window as they can.

The languages cross . . . the voices shrink . . . "Arion . . . and Arion . . . Gladys and Arion . . . lucky man —she's left him . . ."

He wrote me one line:

"She's left me, Anna, and she's kept the ring."

And I wrote: *"Your niece loves you."*

Relatives come and go, up the steps past me and into the house, carrying food, offering help, asking me questions, minding my business. "What are those supposed to be?"

Aunt Lud is trying to keep everyone jolly.

Arion's letters grew shorter until they were only one line, written in a very small hand, cramped in the middle of the page.

"We try not to explode any children—but we don't try too hard, because, God Almighty, this is WAR!"

"Arion the brave soldier," Aunt Lud trills.

"Trust Lud to fight for a lost cause," Uncle Barnard shouts in his stringy voice.

There is dead silence. Someone sobs and runs into the parlor. It sounds like Gemma.

Uncle Barnard in dirty checkered pants, a belt and

suspenders, stumps out onto the porch. "Want to hear a joke, girl?" *Snap*, he snaps his suspender. "You and your potatoes?" His eyes slit, only the black pupils snap at me. *Snap, snap.*

"No, thank you." I lean away from his sour breath.

"Humph! No one in this bloody family has a sense of humor." Uncle Barnard grows red as a baboon's bottom. "And you, Anna, you're a cold one." *Snap.* "You wouldn't recognize a joke from a ham bone. You're worse off than Arion, scared of his own prick." *Snap. Snap.* "You'll be an old maid, mark my words. No man is going to ask you to hot up his bed, you female you! Playing with spuds!" *SNAP!*

Uncle Barnard goose-steps back into the kitchen, all cheeks shaking. "That girl's old enough to be told a few facts. Miss Innocence is!"

"I think she knows."

I try to remember he is Mom's brother. (I will too be hot in bed!) Mom says, "It takes all kinds to make a world." Dad says, "Yeah, but do they have to be related to us?"

More relatives come. More leave.

Arion once wrote:

"Family gives me strange feelings. I am strange feeling."

Later he wrote:

"The evil that is in me . . ."

. . . and said nothing more. That was his last letter to me.

Gemma comes out and sits down beside me. That's

a surprise. "You must have a couple dozen soldier-boy Arions there! Better watch it. Pretty soon that dog's going to be bald."

She's trying to be friendly, but I wish she'd just go away.

"Guess your uncle Arion is pretty special to you, eh!"

Too special for me to talk about! "Yeah, I suppose so." I try to sound very bored and to act busy at the same time. I am working on the scene where Arion and his friend shoot Bart's enemies, making them watch their own deaths, and then rolling them over on their backsides.

". . . too special for you to talk about, eh!" says Aunt Gemma, prying. "I mean otherwise you wouldn't be sitting here—would you?"

Lay off me, Gemma! First it's Uncle Barnard and now it's Gemma! "Guess not," I say.

"I suppose you wish it were he, not me sitting here!" she snaps like Gran.

I look up, surprised.

Then she says, coolly, blowing on her nails, "Been nearly a week now since you took up your new station in life."

"Five days. One day to go," I say, blowing on my nails.

She ignores that, doesn't even say "copycat." "Oh, yes, that's right. You've got the time down pretty pat. . . ."

"TIME!" hollers Gramps from inside. "Did somebody say 'time'? *Was ist die Uhr?*"

How did he hear that? "One day, Gramps," I call. "Only one day left."

"One day? One day you say, little Anna? Is that all?"

"Yes, Gramps."

I turn to Gemma, "Why aren't we meeting him at the station?"

"It's better to wait at home. The government suggested we wait at home."

"Why?"

"Because."

Some answer!

"Anna, I know how it feels."

"What feels?"

"I used to know a boy . . ."

Oh, groan. Not that. I don't want Gemma's secrets.

"And he was older than me . . . and . . . and I had . . . a crush."

Oh, no. Don't go on, please don't go on. Everything's bad enough just the way it is. Don't help it. I hate you, Gemma, I really do. I hate you and I want to hate you.

". . . Course we weren't related!"

"What?"

"I did have a crush on him—true—but we weren't kinfolk."

"Why you BEAST, Gemma!"

"Well, it's true, isn't it? The Bible says . . ."

"The BIBLE. I don't care what that moldy old book of yours says. What's the Bible got to do with US—with Arion and me? We're just . . . family . . . we're   79 just . . . friends . . . he's just my favorite uncle . . . that's ALL he is!"

"I have eyes, little girl—and I'm not the only one has eyes for what you're up to—how many girls you know would sit nearly a whole week in one spot waiting for a favorite uncle? Everybody can see it plain. The Bible says it's a SIN. . . ."

"What are you talking about? I wasn't ten years old when he left us."

"Well, you're nearly fourteen now. . . ."

"GODDAMN YOU, GEMMA. I HATE YOU. AREN'T THINGS BAD ENOUGH AROUND HERE WITHOUT YOU ENTERTAINING YOURSELF!"

"REALLY! WELL, I NEVER . . ."

Oh no, oh dear God, please bring Arion home. Please please just leave him alone.

"Why won't everybody just LEAVE ME ALONE!" I'm sobbing again, damn her, "DAMN YOU TO HELL!"

Gemma stares at me like she's swallowed a frog.

"Come come, come away, Gemma, *ma petite chou-fleur*," Gran soothes. "Come away now."

"I was only trying to help. . . ." Gemma whimpers. "I'm only ever trying to help, to save her a lot of grief. I was only trying to be a Good Christian. Oh, Mama, why can't I ever help anyone, like Ginny can? . . ."

"Now, now, tush, tush *ma petite chou-fleur*." Gran gives me a filthy look. ME! Gran giving ME the filthy look—and before I know what I'm doing, I'm hitting Gran, pounding her on her little back, on the back of her tiny head, and yelling, "Why is everybody so UGLY around here? UGLY UGLY UGLYUGLY, everybody's turned UGLY and NASTY all of a sudden."

Uncle Hud pulls me off and holds me against his chest. "Hush-a, hush-a now, my child, my Pet."

What kind of a place IS this? You can't trust anybody to be themselves. Gemma's crying and a full-grown man like Hud is crooning "Hush-a, hush-a" and calling me— ME—his Pet! And me—what about me?! I can't ever trust myself . . . imagine me, hitting poor old Gran! Oh, Arion . . .

Homecoming Minus 1

"How much time left?" Gramps calls.

"Not long now, Dad," Uncle Hud answers, rubbing his bald head.

"Less than a day now, Dad," Aunt Lud echoes.

LESS. Less than a day? Is that all!

Ginny tweaks my hair and trips on past. "If you're going to cry, Pet, sit in the shade so it doesn't show."

I move into the narrow shade offered by the corner post.

"Exactly how much longer?" Gramps calls.

"A day less seven minutes, old man," growls Uncle Barnard.

"Don't answer that way, boy!" Gran snaps. "*Ce n'est pas gentil.* Don't you tell *ton père* the wrong time. Tell him *quelle heure il est.*"

"In his last letter Arion said sometimes he wondered who he was," Uncle Barnard says.

"What did he mean by that?" asks Gemma.

"How should I know? He said sometimes he wondered if he was anybody."

"Well, at least that's understandable," says Aunt Lud.

"Understandable! How do you figure that?" barks Uncle Hud.

"He also wrote," Uncle Hud grumbles, "that sometimes he thought he was the only real person in the world."

"How queer." Aunt Lud frowns, perching her gangly legs on the chair rung.

"Queer!" Uncle Hud grunts. "That's the most sensible thing the boy ever said."

"Oh, really, honey?" sings Aunt Lud. "Well, then maybe it's a good sign."

"How long now?" Gramps mumbles.

"Rest and sleep now, Helmut." It's not often Gran calls him by his given name.

"Arion, Arion, Arion," Uncle Barnard mutters. "That's all I hear: Arion, Arion, Arion."

"Dad needs to lie down, Maw," Aunt Lud trills. "Why don't you put him in the bedroom, in the shade, where it's cool? . . ."

"No. No no." Gramps scrambles upright in his chair. "NO!"

"Okay, Dad. Okay." Hud rubs his head.

"*Très bien*, Helmut. *Très bien*," Gran clucks.

"I should not have signed these papers! Like a *Dummkopf* I sign."

"*Nein, mein* husband. *Nein, nein, mein Mann.*"

"I've got to do something about myself, Anna. I don't think I like me."

"You getting over your crush?"

Oh, no. Not Gemma again!

"You can, you know."

"Can what?"

"Get over your raging crush."

Oh, I do hate her. "Haven't you said enough!"

"Apparently not. I'm only trying to help you, Anna. I know that it's hard in your stubborn case for me to . . ."

"IMPOSSIBLE."

"What?"

"I said it's impossible. You're impossible, and it's impossible for you to help—anyone—you devil's instrument you."

"I'll overlook that remark; you don't mean it."

"Oh, yes, I do."

"And let me warn you, there's a lot you have to learn about man's natural nature." Gemma gets a highly religious look on her face. "God's eyes are everywhere," she says, and runs on down the steps.

I watch her running down the path to meet her latest mediocre boyfriend, who's too good for the likes of her. I stand up and shout after them, "I know who taught you all you know about MEN'S NATURAL NATURES!" The gate slaps shut. What pleasure does she get out of finding sin where there is no sin?

There isn't any, is there?

Arion doesn't like her. Maybe he won't even hug her tomorrow. And we'll just see how she likes that.

I can't help remembering the day I keep trying to forget, the day Uncle Arion first told Gramps he was going to war.

"I got to do it, Dad." Arion leaned, braced on the kitchen table.

"Nein!" Gramps almost leapt out of his chair.

"Yes, Dad, I can't help it, Dad." Arion's knuckles whitened on the table edge.

Gramps looked at Arion and then at his own feet. Gran was out in the garden. Ginny and Gemma were out visiting. Gramps and Arion had forgotten me skulking in the corner. Arion was shouting, "I can't help it, Dad. All the guys are going."

"I only wish, *Sohn*—" Gramps laid open his hands.

"It's got nothing to do with wishing, Dad." Arion let go of the table and walked toward me; I shrank back, and he didn't seem to notice. "I'm a Canadian, Dad. Born and—"

"And not bred, *Sohn* . . . not bred . . ." Gramps stood there shaking his head . . . "not bred."

"I'm young, Dad. I'm a young man and a Canadian—besides, how can I not go to war! I ask you that. You answer me that—how can I NOT go to war? If you were in my place would you go?"

"What are you going to tell *ta mère*?"

"Nothing. You tell her for me."

"*Nein.* You're not going to kill Germans!"

"Awh God, Dad, for Christ's sake, Dad—I got no choice!"

(Oh, ohh poor Gramps, poor Gramps is German.)

Gramps' knees buckled and he slumped into the chair like he had been shot. He sat there shaking his head like the whole damn thing was just too unbelievable for him to fall down—like my brother says, a shot deer can stand looking at you before it falls dead.

I ran home and hid in the branches of the big cedar on the riverbank.

The voices are at it in the kitchen again. Uncle Barnard is almost shouting. "Arion made a dumb mistake! Sure I know he's everybody's little wonder boy, but facts is facts." Uncle Barnard loudly passes out revelations like they weren't horse buns. "Sometimes you just got to stand up like a man and say, 'No I'm not going to war for my country nohow.' You got to stand up and be counted as missing. I'm like that. You got to pressurize the government. If the worst comes to the worst, tell them you're a pacifist."

Uncle Hud grunts, "You were just too old and ornery for them to take you, Barnard."

"The trouble with Arion," Uncle Barnard says, "is he doesn't truly comprehend guns and bullets is guns and bullets, and charm is only charm." Uncle Barnard pauses for effect and a pinch of snuff. "Charm don't kill Krauts!"

Everyone looks over at Gramps. "Krauts." The word "Krauts" hangs in the air like the stink of cabbage cooking.

Uncle Barnard just stands there like he's bit and pulled the pin on a grenade and there's no place to throw it but at family.

Gramps snorts, stand up, and leaves the room.

Gran hurries after him, wiping her hands on her apron and making little whimpering sounds like I've never heard her make before.

Doomsday

MORNING

Uncle Arion's homecoming is today. Nobody can hide any longer.

We are having an Indian summer. The sun is burning bright, the river shimmers, mirages quaver on the mud flats, timber slashings toast on the bald mountain patches. When I look up from the bottom step, the sky hurts my eyes. Gran looks like she's been crying and so does Gramps.

Gemma growls, "Can't you get the girl to move? She's blocking the way."

"Leave her be, Gemma," Gramps says.

"I still say it's wrong."

"*Ja*, Gemma, it is wrong not to tell . . . wrong to tell . . . I must warn *das Kind, ja . . . nein . . .* leave her be." Gramps stands stiffly at attention in his best suit.

Gran bends over, brushing fluff off Gramps' pant

leg. It's his one good all-occasion black suit. Gran says busily, without looking up, "Yes, Gemma, let her alone. Why do you pester her?"

I can't believe it! Gran defending me—and against Gemma!

"But Mooooommmmmmmm," wails Gemma.

"Hush. Enough's enough, Gemma. And you, old man, stand still. Stand still, *mon vieux*."

Gramps stands chewing his cud and thinking private thoughts. He hasn't got his false teeth in yet.

"Helmut, stop mashing your gums."

Gramps doesn't have an audience yet; I guess he's saving his crack about who's got the family dentures until everyone arrives. "Emma, Emma, don't fuss."

Gramps just called Gran Emma! And all these years I thought he was yelling "hey Maw." I can hardly believe it. What a day; Gramps calls Gran by her first name, and Gran chastizes Gemma on my behalf. Maybe they are good omens.

Gran stops brushing and straightens up in front of Gramps, looking up at him. She could stand ramrod upright under his armpit with room to spare. They seem so close now, much closer than when he pinches her.

I look away. For a long time I balance, leaning back on my elbows, and stare at the sky, hurting my eyes.

Soon the old farm table Gramps built will groan under the banquet: ham and turkey, salad and stuffed eggs, Uncle Arion's favorite cream puffs—every party trapping but balloons and crepe paper.

The Manx cat takes one look in through the doorway, then turns and marches off, disgusted. Relatives filter in, hushed: Aunt Lud, trying to make light; Aunt Cessy, flicking her round moons like a young girl; Uncle Barnard, eldest boy, strutting like *he's* just come home from the wars. Gran staggers with the heavy turkey platter; Uncle Hud flits sideways, like a dancer, to rescue the turkey, the Blue Willow platter, and Gran. Gemma sucks a cut finger at the sink, but nobody notices her. Mom and Dad sit together on the bench, Dad leaning against the wall, Mom folding napkins. Aunt Lud carries a potato salad that's not turning green. Cousin Alice, blonde and transparent, drifts shyly to a shadowed corner and sets down a plate of happy-for-ever-after cake.

Gramps stands with his back to the window, wetting his lips and sucking his false teeth. There's a lull; everybody's waiting for the joke.

"Was ist die Uhr?" Gramps asks. "And where's my cat?"

"Only a few minutes more, Dad."

Oh, make it longer!

I hurry outside to check on my gift for Arion. I've dragged the bench out on the porch and set all my potato figures on it. There are nineteen Arions now. I have buried porcupine Gladys, pins and all.

The sun has burnt a hole in the sky, a hole in my eyes. When I look over the flats, blind spots like caves pockmark the mountains. The caves vanish, the mountains recede, and my relatives stand in sudden silence. A nervous laugh like an astonished bird breaks flight. Gran in blue, Gramps in black serge, aunts and uncles like paper cutouts, stand shadowless in the high noon. Paper cutout dolls. Cardboard smiles.

Don't let it be now.

"Taxi, taxi, here's the taxi," Cousin Will yells from the gate.

From where I sit I see only the backs of family as they move toward the road, the gate: Aunt Lud's maroon back, Gran's blue back and, when I stand, only a car, its door open, and two strangers in white uniforms standing at the gate . . . and then the path closes up with the bodies of my aunts and uncles and cousins. Only Aunt Cessy stands to the side, wringing her hands.

Nobody says a word until Aunt Cessy's husband, Uncle Jerry, yells for his brother, "Arion, my God! He's here. He's here! The hero's home!" His voice breaks.

I can't see him. Where is he? "Stop crowding. Let me see." I'm the one who cares! They crowd around him at the gate. Gemma's gray back is all I see, patches of Ginny's flowered dress jumping around. I can't see. What do they see? Is he taller? Is he so very, very handsome? Is he looking for me?

"Here he is. Here's the lad," my uncle Hud hollers.

"Make way. Make way. Let the man pass." Cousin Alice's fiancé waves his arms over all their heads.

Cousin Alice glides backward into the grass, Aunt Lud stumbles into Alice, dropping her lace handkerchief. Ginny picks the handkerchief off the tops of the tall grasses while still tripping backward out of the way of a brother's big feet. My aunts and uncles and cousins are crowded together. Then, they scatter as if exploded.

And there he is. My Arion. White as the moon. One of the white strangers is my uncle. He has no cap on; his hair isn't golden. Are his eyes blue? And he is so thin. A stranger in a white uniform guides him; Arion too wears white. He walks stiffly and so slowly that Gramps can easily lead the way, stepping backward in front of him. And he's stooped. And he can't be my uncle. His eyes look only at the clouds.

Why isn't he in his army uniform?

Where are all his medals?

Gemma, sidestepping beside Gramps, trips on one of the whitewashed stones bordering Gran's garden; Uncle Hud tramps on the parsley. The sun blinks through the plum tree leaves. Arion, a white statue, is guided scuffling up the garden path. Gran clings to his arm, crying, snatching away her tears with the corner of her apron, pulling him toward the steps. My gran. The other one, the strange man in white, carries one suitcase. Gramps stumbles with the other suitcase, pulling it out of the grasp of uncles and cousins, of younger men. My gramps. I stand at the foot of the stairs watching my uncle coming this way. I never did expect him to come back suntanned and smelling of the perfumes of foreign countries. But I didn't expect this either. He turns in a goose step, arms straight at his sides, legs scissoring—and stops at eye level. I look into his face—his eyes are still blue—but he doesn't seem to see me. That's it! That's all that's wrong with him; he's blind! Oh, poor Arion, poor Arion, you're blind, your days as dark as Gran's kitchen. I clap my hands at him, "I'm here. Uncle Arion, it's me, it's me." Never mind, I think, I'll be your eyes.

"Now, now, Anna." Aunt Cessy pats me.

"Non, non," Gran shakes her head.

I reach for his face, but he turns and I touch an ear.

He can't be deaf too, can he? Sure he can, he's deaf and blind; that's all that's wrong with him.

Never mind, I'll be your ears.

I pull at his sleeve and whisper, "I'll be your eyes and your ears." He doesn't climb the stairs, but I step back and up one step so that I come to his chin.

And he looks down at me and through me.

I drop his sleeve and his arm dangles. He's forgotten me. How could he? Me! Maybe it's false, his arms are false; maybe his legs are false, they move so stiffly. If he doesn't remember me . . . he might be all false. A spy, a false uncle.

I step back down and reach out and touch his leg. It is real. He is all real—and he's forgotten me. How could he?

"Uncle Arion, Uncle Arion! It's me—grown. Anna grown up. Your Anna. Oh, please."

He isn't smiling. He doesn't know me! He doesn't know me!

He isn't smiling and he doesn't know me!

He doesn't know me. And he isn't blind and he isn't deaf. And I hate him.

No one moves, then the Manx cat hisses, and all the cardboard figures come to life, rushing back in. Some of the men in the family pound him cautiously on the back. "Welcome, soldier, son, brother." The women plant kisses on his cheeks, his mouth . . . little kisses on his neck . . . then fall back again with fluttery hands . . . weeping. Cousin Alice, Aunt Lud, and Cessy, Mom . . . uncles . . . weeping. I look at my uncle Arion again. Who is he?

Then I bump against Gramps' pant leg and bump the suitcase he's carrying, Arion's suitcase. Will it be full of souvenirs for me? A fancy handkerchief? Grenades? I look at him balanced on the first step. Who is this man? Where is my uncle Arion?

The statue mounts, one foot up one step—Arion used to bound up! The Manx cat sits on the doorsill, blocking the path.

"Ssssssst ssssst scat, cat," Gramps hisses. It scats.

What about me? Nobody else sat here a whole week waiting! What about me?

"Watch the doorsill, *Sohn*," Gramps calls.

"Up, up," twitters Gran.

I care. What about me? I care . . . too.

Uncle Arion farts just as he steps over the doorjamb. And Uncle Barnard, who has stayed in the kitchen feeding his face and swilling beer, crows, "Rah rah, the hero returns," and waves a stuffed egg in the air.

AFTERNOON

It's an hour since I ran home, past Cousin Will who was leaning on the gatepost with his face turned away. I couldn't have said hello anyway. I ran home, to be alone.

What am I doing here in my pink room lying on my frilly bed? Who am I? I feel the satin bedspread slippery cool on my legs. I've missed it; a frill tickles my nose—but I don't scratch. Who was I when I kept a vigil, ran over bombed-out fields in my dreams, scrambled under barbed wire, sidestepped land mines? Who was that girl?

Lying in my pink and stifling room, I roll over and stare at the jungle of flowers on my linoleum floor.

I ran. But not before I had swept my gift for Arion onto the floor: potato bodies everywhere underfoot; Uncle Hud slipping, Aunt Lud stepping high, Gemma crushing one under her heel.

I threw myself on my bed and cried and cried and only now do I stop when I hear Marsh coming upstairs to his room.

But it isn't Marsh, it's Dad. He opens the door and fills the doorway, handsome in his suit, his hair afire in the light from my brother's room. I fling myself across the room and into his arms and cry and cry, and he cries with me, even though the men in our family don't do that. Will, too, was crying at the gate; I know that now.

"Why, Dad? Why?"

"I'm sorry. I'm sorry, Anna my love. I know it hurts."

"What's wrong, Dad, what's wrong with Uncle Arion?"

Dad strokes me, my hair, my shoulders, my arms. "I'm sorry, my girl. I wish war had noble ends . . . that men came home covered in glory and medals . . . but sometimes they die. . . ."

"But not Uncle Arion. He didn't die."

". . . Their bodies sometimes . . . but at other times, like your uncle now . . . Anna, do you want to hear this?!"

"Yes, yes."

". . . Like your uncle now . . . it's just their minds die."

"No no no."

"Awh, honey, I'm sorry. So sorry." He rocks me. "My baby . . . we thought you guessed . . . a little. . . . It's my fault, my fault. . . ."

I plug my ears with the heels of my hands. "No, Dad, no. I won't let it be true." But I hear him.

"There are miracles, Anna. Sometimes love, hope, alone . . ."

"No, no, Daddy, I planned on a miracle. I hoped so hard. I already did that."

As Dad cries I watch his tears changing course, confused among the red stubble of his growing whiskers. And I try to concentrate on that, on tears like water, like streams running through stubble, down the mountain through slashings . . . oh, I won't let it be true!

Potato Soldier

It can't be true. My uncle Arion isn't this half man. From what I hear, he just sits on his new chair at the window. Sits looking at the glass.

I overhear Mom and Aunt Lud talking in our kitchen. From here, the top step on our porch, I could lean back and see them doing the dishes. I don't; I just sit and listen in.

"Sits looking at the window." Aunt Lud twists the dish towel into the glass till it squeals.

"Sitting? Still just sitting?" Mom swishes the soapy water.

"Umhm, sitting."

"Does he smoke?"

"No, doesn't smoke."

"He used to smoke heavily."

"Hmm. A regular chimney, our Arion. Just sits now, though."

"A shame. Terrible shame . . ."

"Mind you, May, I say it's just temporary. . . ."

"Only sits, you say . . ."

"Mmm, in his chair . . ."

I move down to the end of the bottom step but I know the end of the sentence . . . "looking at the window glass." Only, I don't know that for myself. I haven't been over to see him since the Great Day. I don't want to go . . . anywhere . . . to do . . . anything. I sit on the porch at our house, staring straight ahead like Arion—but I see. I see the backwoods. There are Indian graves in that wild backwoods beyond the marsh, the field, our tamed backyard. I see a crow sitting on our fence post, cawing stupidly. Wish I were deaf and blind.

Marsh comes up, carrying the short gaff. "It's the end of the salmon run, Sis, and nearly the last day we have hopes of finding some spawners with any silver left. In a couple of days all we'll have left is the rotters on the bank."

I wrinkle my nose.

"Making faces, I see, that's heartening," he says. "Can't you just taste the roe," and he tongues his lip, tempting me, trying to get me thinking of roast fish eggs sprinkled with salt.

I snort. "I don't want to be heartened."

"Suit yourself then," he says and leaves. Boy slinks off behind him, feeling low and guilty. And so he should!

Mom walks up behind me. I can sense her there even though I don't look up. She's been doing that for several days now, walking up behind me and then walking away, saying nothing.

"Anna, what you're doing isn't good for you," she says, like maybe I haven't been eating my vegetables or swallowing my cod-liver oil pills.

"Oh, Mom," I groan, disgusted.

She's a shy woman and she goes away. I feel uneasy about upsetting her—but not sorry. Sending Uncle Arion home like that was the dirtiest punch God could have thrown.

Gemma comes crunching up the gravel driveway. She pauses and sniffs a fading flower. How phony can you get! "Wrapped in gloom, I see," she says as she passes—says it without any bite. "We all are, you know."

Not like me! Not like me! I want to yell after her, "WHAT DO YOU THINK OF YOUR GOD NOW?"

She drops a paper bag; inside are all my bruised potatoes. I close it quick.

She only stays a minute. On her way out, I say, "I've been tricked."

"Oh." She stops cold. "And who's to blame! I told you Arion wasn't like you pictured him. You just forgot."

"FORGOT! He was never anything like . . . like . . . this thing they've sent back to us!"

"He's just an ordinary man, Anna, needing time to heal. Why aren't you a bit more practical, give him time. Poor man, the Lord could be balm for his soul, if he'd only let himself believe, repent, suffer, be washed in the blood of the lamb."

"YOU LEAVE HIM ALONE, GEMMA! You just leave him alone."

"My, my, I thought you didn't want him. Not that he's yours."

"It's the rest of us who have to repent—you HEATHEN you!"

"Now, now, simmer down, Anna. You're not making sense, and I'm just trying to tell you that he's a perfectly ordinary mortal man, a kitchen-garden variety human being, a thoroughly common man. . . ."

"Well, he wasn't BEFORE!"

"So he is NOW," she says triumphantly. "And he was too before!" She gets up to go. "You're not the only one misses him, you know. I'm his sister after all."

I give her a dark look.

"Just who do you think kept his egg-collection cabinet dusted all these years?"

Not Gemma, surely?

"And put straw flowers in his room?"

She leaves me sitting here.

After a while I open the bag again. The potatoes have aged, they aren't growing shoots yet, but they are wrinkled like old apples, and smelly.

By the time Aunt Lud, gaunt in her straight maroon dress, bones sticking out at the lacy neck, comes up the path on the arm of tiny Uncle Hud, dressed in forest green like a foreign leprechaun, I'm feeling ugly, and sorry too.

"You seem to like sitting on steps, Anna," she says sweetly. Always sweetly. I don't answer. Why does she always have to be so sweet? They go inside.

I can hear Mom scurrying across the linoleum, boiling up the tea water, and no doubt laying out the plates of cold turkey sandwiches and crackers larded with slabs of cheese. The local relatives and the out-of-towners who remain come and go between the two houses, ours and Arion's. "Hello, Anna, you seen the Manx cat? Gramps is looking for it," Cousin Alice asks, smiling sadly.

I see Uncle Barnard in the distance, coming up on the river side of the road, along the boardwalk. He isn't marching or swinging his cane. Instead he is walking with his head down, like he's searching for something underneath, peering through the wooden slats, or maybe just watching his feet. When he reaches my shoulder, he leans over. "Where's your black armband, girl?" he growls.

And when I look up I see it's no joke, that he's angry with me. He's wearing a black band. He hisses, "Show some respect," and goes on up the stairs.

I stare after him.

Aunt Cessy plops down beside me. I don't look up. She's wearing shorts and her fried-eggs sweat shirt and bell rings on her middle toes. "Anna, I thought you knew. I thought somebody must have warned you. Nobody here tells the kids anything."

I don't answer. I look at her legs, they're freckled.

"Listen, Anna, I'm going to tell you something."

"And if I say don't?" Her kneecaps are dimpled.

"I'm going to anyways."

"Don't." Her eyes are green, flecked tawny.

"I worked in the plywood mill one summer when I was your age."

"I know that." Her skin is freckled but creamy. Her chest jutts out, like a cliff, drops to her lap.

"There was a girl there. Everybody was mean to her or they ignored her. When they ignored her, she must have felt lucky."

"You were mean too?"

"I kept my distance."

"So?" Why does she wear silly sweat shirts?

"So I could have befriended her. That plywood mill is one of the grayest, most dismal places on the face of this earth. You know how gray it looks from the canal, built low on the hillside and exposed to the north. It's worse yet inside. There are no windows, only skylights choked with sawdust. I was lonely too, but she was lonelier and all I did was pull my hat over my ears and walk by her without speaking."

"So? It's no crime." Does she have to wear her shorts so short? And her nails so long? And those bell rings from India on her toes!

"Isn't it, Anna? She hung herself. She hung herself from a water pipe in the basement of her apartment."

"Oh . . . well I'm sorry about that, but surely you aren't saying you killed her."

"No. I'm too sensible to say that. But I didn't help her live, Anna. You must see that."

"What's that got to do with me?"

"Well, nothing maybe—I can't find an exact parallel for your crime."

"Crime! You sound like Gemma."

"Don't be so hard on Gemma."

"Hmmmph."

"So maybe you just found out about suffering.

Tough beans. Life is only life, after all. And only you can make it worse than it is in truth."

Snort.

"Oh, Anna. Anna, my pigeon. If only we could . . . somehow . . . spare each other." She puts a creamy freckled arm around me, and I cave in my chest so that she doesn't accidentally touch me. What can I say? What can I say?

"I think I'd better go along home now, Anna."

I don't stop her. After she leaves I get up and walk down the steps, and lift the lid off the garbage can, not bothering to hold my nose against the stench. I just breathe in all the ugly smells and open the potato bag and take one last look at my Arions, before I drop them into the can. I was childish making them. They are only old potatoes, after all.

Potato Niece

The summer holidays are almost over. Sal Anne's back,
and so is my brother's friend Joe. I'm glad to see Sal
Anne, and Joe's okay, I guess.

Three fence posts between our yard and the back
field are decorated with black crows, tipping in the
wind and facing upwind to keep their feathers from
ruffling.

Won't it ever go away?

I'm sitting on our steps at home again—out of
habit—it doesn't feel good, or safe here anymore. Really
I just don't care about anybody. To hell with Aunt Cessy
and her crazy stories. I just don't care. I agree with what
Arion wrote in one of his last letters to me.

"So this is living? Join the war and see Death."

One crow flies off.

I never stopped writing him, long after he stopped writing me I kept on writing, not caring that I couldn't mail those letters since nobody would give me his address. Fat lot of good it did me. . . .

Jeez, I'm getting to be a real weeping ninny—I can hardly stand myself these days.

Two crows fly off together.

"Okay, Sis, snap out of it!"

"What?"

"You heard me." Marsh pounds on down the steps past me in his hip-waders. "Come on, Boy. You're not responsible for Miss Gloom." Boy bounds off.

I'm so goddamn mad. "Then who IS?" I yell. "Who is responsible?"

"You."

Me? Since when?

"You." He turns around and bounds off backward in his heavy waders. "You're responsible for you. YOU YOU YOU." The scar on his cheek is fiery red.

First Gemma, then Mom, Aunt Cessy. And now him too. I sit back down. "Oh, yeah. Who says so . . . yeah, yeah, Marshbog?" But I can't put much feeling into the taunt, and I don't think he heard me.

Nobody hears me. Except Uncle Barnard. But surprisingly he just walks on by, touching my shoulder gently as he passes. Gently. I can't believe it. It's enough to make me cry—anything is enough to make me burst out bawling.

Gemma comes into the yard. "Seen your uncle Barnard?"

"Sure. Gone inside."

Gemma hesitates. I try not to look inviting.

"Your uncle Barnard told us a bad joke."

"That's news! And don't forget, he's your relation too."

"You're cruel, Anna."

"ME cruel?"

"You're acting cruel. I think you don't know how to suffer."

I just look at her.

"Well, maybe that's not true—but you are thoughtless—like your Arion." Gemma bobs her head emphatically, satisfied. "I'm not finished." Gemma moves away against the wall. "The joke your uncle Barnard told was about a young soldier. . . . It seems he'd been given this grenade by his instructor, and the instructor says, 'You take this grenade, son, and you pull the pin,' he says, 'and then, son, you count to ten—and whatever you do, my boy, don't be havin' it in your hand after the count of ten.' So the soldier boy he takes that grenade." Gemma stopped. "Well, we were all of us too shocked to cut Barnard off . . . everyone is feeling so exhausted and so helpless these days and, well, we all couldn't quite believe it was happening. So your uncle Barnard—you know how hard it is to stop him . . . and well I guess we half expected Arion to speak up and get him to shut up . . . of course Arion doesn't speak now—and so Barnard kept right on . . .'The soldier boy bit the pin,' he says, 'and counted to eight and then he shoved it between his legs and threw up his hands and yelled, "Look, Maw, no hands!" ' "

Oh, no.

"And . . . and . . . and then he"—Gemma chokes and covers her face with her hand—"Barnard, he started laughing and he couldn't stop. . . ."

And Gemma runs off up the stairs, unable to finish. I don't know what to do. I certainly should help her, but I can't . . . I just can't comfort Gemma.

I just sit.

A little while later Gemma comes back out with her arm around Uncle Barnard. I look up sideways as they pass and see how Uncle Barnard has his hat pulled down to hide that he's been crying. I move over to let them pass.

Gemma looks happy. She's a better person than I am these days.

Mom comes out and stands over me, staring after them. She looks down at me and snaps, "I've had just about enough of you. You think you're the only one who has anything to be sorry for. Well, they're both my brothers!"

I feel sick. Poor Mom, Arion's her brother. And Cousin Will was crying at the gate when I ran past him.

I don't want them hurting. I don't want any of us hurting. I just want it to stop.

To keep from crying I set out the facts:

1. Uncle Arion went off to the war, and when he came back he wasn't a boy any longer.

2. I've been through my own small war, and I guess I'm not the girl I once was.

Laid out like that it looks simple, but it's not. Because now Uncle Arion isn't a boy—and he's not a man either. He's a potato man. I blink back the tears.

Marsh and Boy come up the driveway. Boy comes running ahead to lick my face, whining. I say, "Everything's going to be all right, Boy." But it isn't.

It seems so wrong that I can care this much and yet be healthy, not be the one in a wheelchair. They tell me he is in a wheelchair now, because Uncle Hud put him there for Gran's convenience . . . and against Gran's wishes.

"Here." Marsh drops a packet in my lap.

"What is it?"

He stands back, watching me. I undo the string.

There are six letters—all addressed to my brother and all from Uncle Arion. Marsh never TOLD me. Why not! They're in order, and I can see by the dates that all of them were written after the time Arion stopped writing me:

"Please check, Marsh, and see how my ex-fiancée Gladys is keeping."

Then he wrote about his capture:

"I flew low. I crashed. I was the only survivor."

He wrote as if he were the pilot, but I know he was only a foot soldier.

"I walked away from the burning plane and kept on walking not knowing the country or the planet. Then I was on an airstrip and I wondered if this was Holland. I walked around the corner of a hangar and nearly bumped into a guard. He didn't see me, and I hid till night. Then in the dark, I climbed a wire fence and walked off into the open fields. I saw the Big Dipper and knew I was on this earth. I walked until I was tired and then I lay down and hid for the night in a copse of trees. At dawn I waited for a farmer or a priest, like they told us to. It was a farmer I hailed. He fed me and sent for the priest. The priest prayed and sent for the Germans. They came and took me away. I lived in a barbed-wire camp, on turnip soup, and on lucky days I got a potato. I saw a young German guard eating a piece of bread once. I dropped to my knees and begged. 'You have my blue eyes, can I have your bread?' I even remembered the German word for bread; I looked up into his face and he was my mirror. And my mirror looked away. I was one of many. What else could he do?"

The next three letters spoke of life in Germany. I wanted to cry again; I looked away, at the river that mirrored the sky; for the postmark was Great Britain.

"I met a family Aryan-pure, of the purified blood pool. But the Russians arrived and the family locked the door of their apartment and decided to swallow poison, the children first. The oldest boy was fourteen, old enough to argue; he argued with his parents. He told them, 'I do not want to die.' I heard him scuffle with his dad. And I heard them scream. I heard the boy gasp, 'I want . . . I want . . . to . . . live.' But he died."

He described a streetcar ride, a carload of Canadians, Americans, Englishmen, and Germans and Russians too. All pressed close together, rubbing against each other, elbowing, fidgeting, the men grinning at the *Deutschland* girls and belching and winking and passing gas.

"There's hardly a child in Germany who hasn't heard of a relative or neighbor hanging himself. Children all over Germany climb hopefully up to attics dying to catch a glimpse of a foot swinging between the lines of laundry. Children will grow up understanding *Selbstmord*. 'Suicide, suicide,' they will chant as they jump rope."

He played with the words in the shape of a scaffold.

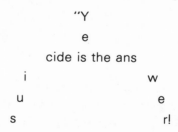

```
       "Y
         e
   cide is the ans
 i                 w
   u                 e
   s                 r!
```

At least in dying they know they lived."

All the letters were dated after the war, but he wrote as if it were still wartime.

"We Germans are more afraid of Nazism and of our neighbors and our own brothers than we are of the enemy. The enemy is not as free to walk through my door as my good neighbor and my family."

He drew a picture of a hand pointing to a door on <u>110</u> which there was a swastika and a Star of David.

"Do not believe what Jewish friends tell you. We did not—could not—do that to little children!"

The letterhead is the same on all envelopes, a hospital in England.

"All at once, all over the country, printed notices were sent to the families of retarded children, telling them the date that their sons and daughters had died. Later little parcels marked 'Clothing and Personal Effects' were returned to the families."

I fold the letters and hand them back. Marsh won't look at me.

"Why didn't anybody tell me?"

"I guess . . . maybe . . . I . . . we . . . thought we would never have to."

"What do you mean? You knew he had to come home sometime."

"No. And if he did, I guess everybody hoped it would be . . . different."

"Oh, yeah, sure. So everybody knew but me, eh?"

"Well, nobody wanted it this way. Do you think anybody WANTED it this way!!"

"*You* should have told me."

"I tried . . . but I couldn't make myself do it. Mom and Dad tried too. You didn't want to know. And you stopped Gemma from warning you. You know that."

"But they told *you*."

"No. Does anybody around here ever tell kids anything? I knew when I got the letters."

I sulk.

Marsh says, "And then I didn't get any more letters."

I look at my hands prattling on my knees.

Marsh continues, "Yesterday I overheard Gramps
saying they wrote him and Gran to sign the papers for
the cure. Uncle Barnard said Gramps never should have
signed, that they butchered Arion's mind. Dad said shock
therapy was a good thing and couldn't do that. Aunt
Cessy said Arion tried to commit suicide—that his body
didn't make it but his mind did. Aunt Lud said if it was
anything at all, it was just battle fatigue and very, very
temporary. Gemma tried to blame Gladys."

I look up to agree. But Marsh isn't looking at me. He
goes on talking.

"Uncle Hud said that Arion wasn't well to begin
with and that the war tore him apart and made him turn
bad inside and feel guilty for everything forever. I don't
know. Why has this darn family always got more answers
than there are questions? I don't know. I just say he's a
brave soldier and it's his mind they crippled instead of
a leg or an arm or something."

I plug my ears and hug Boy. Marsh gets up.

"Where are you going?" I ask.

"To see Arion. You coming?"

I don't answer.

"For God's sake, why don't you just hammer down
the lid."

I look at him.

"Hammer down the coffin lid, Sis."

I can't visit. Not yet.

"He's still alive, you know. You're not giving him a

chance." And he stomps off. Boy follows, naturally.

I feel so sorry for them, Arion, my brother, Mom, Dad, Cousin Will, all of them, and so very sorry for Gran and Gramps—but I can't tell them that. I can't say it out loud. What's the matter with me?!

All of Us

"Hello, Anna."

"Oh, Aunt Lud."

"Enjoying the sun, I see."

Humph. I know there's no longer any reason for me to sit on porches. There's no sun shining, and I huddle in my thin blouse. There are no crows on the back field fence posts. Aunt Lud blunders up our steps, tripping on the landing. She pauses for a moment to sort herself out. I feel her looking down at the top of my head. A cloud of perfumed cow settles over me. "I'm in to see your mom for a second, then off for a nice little visit with our Arion. It must make you feel good to see your uncle Arion?"

I look at her, amazed.

"Hardly lost a hair on his head, the lucky man. Most of our family's going bald by his age—the men, that is."

She pats her own thinning crown. "Yes, all bald by thirty-five, and yet his hair is as thick as a boy's! Ah, well that's life." She lumbers on in.

Can you believe it!

Marsh appears from around the corner of the house.

"Do you know what Aunt Lud just said?"

"Uh-huh."

"She said Arion's LUCKY not to be bald."

"Yeah, I heard her."

"LUCKY, she said LUCKY not to be BALD."

"You're like Aunt Lud."

". . . That's what she said, 'Arion is lucky' "—I look at Marsh—"What did you say?"

"I said you're like Aunt Lud."

"What! ME? You're as crazy as she is. What's happened to Arion is CRUEL, and she calls it LUCKY! Not me. I'm not like that." Of course, I'm yelling again, and Mom sticks her head out the side window, frowning. "I never said lucky. . . ." my voice trails off.

"Yes, you are like her," Marsh repeats, "but not exactly."

"What's that supposed to mean?!"

"You and Aunt Lud, the two of you, you're always pretending. But you're worse. She at least talks to Arion—you don't go near him."

It's the truth. I glare.

"Well *do* you?"

"Do I what?"

"Go near him?"

". . . No . . ."

Marsh sits down and takes my hand. "Yesterday, Sis,

I went to see him. That was only my second time. It's no joke seeing him like that. No fun. I can promise you that much." He sighs.

"What did he do?"

"Do? Nothing. He doesn't do a thing. Just sits."

"That's awful. Doesn't he talk at all?"

"No, he won't speak, but who knows that he isn't hearing—he mightn't be listening—but his ears are there and it only stands to reason, since they say he isn't deaf and he obviously isn't blind or dead, that he's more alone if nobody talks to him."

"What do you . . . talk about?"

"You. I told him about you."

"You had no business . . . what did you say about me?"

"Just about old times . . . and the fun we used to have—"

"And what else? . . ."

". . . How you miss him."

Oh. I hear a catch in Marsh's throat. We sit in silence.

And then Marsh gives me a jog. "Hey Sis. Hey Sis. Still waters run—not deep—?" He's crying now too. . . . "Still waters run . . ."

"STUPID!" we shriek together—Arion's old quip. And Marsh pushes me off the end of the step and I drag him with me and we roll together in the grass with Boy wagging his tail and maneuvering his butt trying to sit on the two of us at once . . . and I remember how it was tusseling with Arion.

Mom pokes her head out the window and the two of

us look up and see her strange expression—confusion battling relief—and we laugh some more, because she looks so funny. And Boy barks the whole time. I know Mom's going to tell Dad about us when they're alone in bed tonight. And maybe he will half smile and whisper sadly in her ear, "My poor little Mayflower."

Uncle Arion, I can imagine you sitting at Gran and Gramps' kitchen window staring at the surface of the glass. Oh, Arion, I can see you sitting there on the porch where you have been put out, young Arion, like an old man, to take the sun, the sun shining through your frizzy hair. Arion, Arion, you don't crack jokes or spout crazy nonsense verse or even pop your knuckles anymore. Girls aren't anywhere in your empty world. And where does that leave me? Your long legs are grown thin, your great stride that I ran to keep time with is now a shuffle. Your hands no longer prattle on your knees, but lie upside down playing dead in your lap. Your eyes don't roll in your head when a pretty girl passes—they just roll. And where does that leave me?

"Hello, Uncle Arion," I say. "Good to see you." And he says—what does he say? Of course, I'm forgetting, he says nothing. What he doesn't say is what I've been waiting to hear: "Why, Anna, what a beauty you've grown into." No, I know what he'll say if I visit. I know. He'll say, "You know there's only one person I'd rather see than my old girl friend and that's you, Anna." I stop myself. Oh, yeah! Oh, sure, Anna, that's real believable. You're losing your grip on fantasy old girl, you old toad. That's all guff—you're losing your daydream touch.

"Hey Sis." 117

Huh. "Oh, my God, Marsh, you've brought him!" Uncle Arion, thin, sticklike, and black in his graduation suit, just stands there. Marsh has walked him over here. Very slowly, and now he's mounted the first step and stands four steps below me, level with my eyes. He stares right over my head. His hands hang at his sides. Oh, Uncle Arion, oh, Arion. Arion. My brother gives him a shake.

"Say hello, Arion," Marsh's voice is sharp, commanding. "Say hello to your Anna, Arion."

"Hello, Arion," I say. Arion salutes. Salutes!

Marsh says, "Say hello to your niece." Marsh tugs at him.

Arion steps up a step. "Hell . . . o neee . . . sssss."

Another step, closer. Oh, take him away, take him away.

"Hello, Uncle Arion, how nice to see you." I'm looking at his knees, staring at the knees of his old high-school graduation suit. So I stand up. Marsh picks up Arion's limp arm and drapes it over my shoulder, and I start crying and can't stop. Arion doesn't bother to pick up the other arm. And then, unbelievably, Arion, soldier home from the wars, on seeing his beloved niece, speaks for the first time.

"Don't cry nee . . . sss," he begins, but then the arm slips from my shoulder and passes back into his new lost self. There was just this flicker of comprehension, as if crying is a thing he could understand, dry weeping he knows well. Nothing more . . .

Marsh says, "Let's go home now, Arion," and turns him around carefully.

I watch them walk off, Arion stupidly, blindly stepping, lifting, dropping, and dragging each foot . . . in its
out-of-date dress shoe . . . leffft riiight leffft riiight.

My eyes follow them to the end of our drive. His
pant cuffs are above his ankle socks, but his pants hang
from his hips, his haunches are flat like an old man's.
He's twenty-two, and he's dressed like a boy. Marsh leans
against him, guiding him; Arion does not lean on Marsh
but marches at attention turning at the gate in a surprising goose step, German march step, down the path till
he's hidden by the sentinal poplars.

The next day I'm out, just walking the boardwalks
by the riverbank, when I turn and see tiny Gran, small in
the distance, wheeling her son-parcel Arion onto the
porch.

There's the feel of rain in the air now but no sign of
any falling; yet summer is over.

Tomorrow. Maybe tomorrow. Or the next day.
Then I'll visit.

I cross to the barbed-wire fence stetched along the
river side of Gran and Gramps' field. At last I've made
it this far, to the fence. From here I can see him just as
Gran left him—well bundled, sitting in his chair on the
porch for his daily constitutional. I can see only his pro-
file, the hawk of his nose. He's been put out to air, facing
the leafless plum trees. He sits staring west, in the direction he's been placed. Later Gramps or Gran will come
out and rotate him. He could see me if he'd turn his head
just a little toward the river, and then look out of those
sea-blue eyes of his. But he doesn't turn. And suddenly I'm holding on to the fence wires and screaming,

"I WON'T COME, NOT UNTIL YOU ASK FOR ME. Not until you ask for me."

Marsh runs up behind me. Boy runs around and around me in circles, whimpering.

I can't. I can't.

"What are you doing, Sis—that's barbed wire for Christ's sake, your hands are bleeding all over my shoes. . . ."

"I can't. I can't go to him. . . ."

"I know, Sis, I know . . ."

I let go of the wire; I feel his arms around me; I feel him turning me.

Of course I will go back someday to Gran and Gramps'—and Arion's. And everything will be the same.

"Come, Sis, that's right . . . come with me." He pats my bloody hands with a shirttail.

Uncle Arion will become a fixture, a fact, like Gramps' growing old, like Gran's arthritis in her fingers and hips. Gran will still be mixing Gramps' salt and pepper together and he'll call it sand to annoy her and he'll joke about family dentures again, mortifying both Gemma and Gran in public. He'll tell Marsh and me fish stories even though we've outgrown them.

"Keep walking, Sis."

It will still be very dark in the kitchen, and Uncle Arion will sit at the window in his new chair opposite Gramps so they can both be in the light.

"Just keep on walking, Sis."

Gramps will pinch Gran as she sails past him into the pantry, and there will be a cold draft and the smell of Limburger cheese when she opens the door. And no one will use the musty parlor reserved for guests. My twin aunts will continue courting in the kitchen . . . the river will flood and the floods retreat and the fish spawn in fall to battle up the canal every spring into the open sea. And we will never be the same again—none of us.

Someday I guess I'll go back.

"Come, Sis, we're almost home."

But not yet. I can't go there. Yet.